Faetality

BY

YSADORA SONDERLING

FAETALITY

First edition. February 14, 2026.

Copyright © 2026 Ysadora Sonderling.

ISBN: 978-1763687479

Written by Ysadora Sonderling.

To Stribi, for doing so much to promote my career.

Chapter One

I am not the hero of this story. Hel, I could never be anyone's hero. If lives depended on me, well, those poor bastards.

Bayton was a funny kind of city, it had grown in size but not mentality, still playing at a small country town. It was full of sleaze and judgement, which was given out in spades to all and sundry. I revelled in the first and bore the second, but then, what else was a faery to do?

Crushing my cigarette into the nearest bin, I quit my navel gazing to cross the street, trying to jump over the puddles of brown sludge left by a smattering of rain. My boots had recently sprung a leak. Scraps of bleached blonde hair flew in the bitter wind that now threatened to tear my coat from me. The remains of my last high were beginning to fade out, making the reality of a cold Bayton night loom ominously. I idly tried to restrain my hair under a scarf, but even the thickest faerylocks were being thrown about wildly in this weather.

Ahead lay the den of my one and only dealer, Stevie, who was grandmaster of the area and would gladly take the few scraps of money I had made today in exchange for a better high than the average given. Think of it as a frequent buyer deal, and it always helped that Stevie had a bit of a crush on me. I knocked on the quaint little red door and waited in sight of the discreet cameras for someone to answer. Eventually the inner bolt was retracted slowly, and the door quickly creaked open to reveal a giant of a man.

'Hiya Jojo, how goes it?'

'Mmrrmmm m'kay Jessie. Busy. Lossa work,' replied the door and standover man only known as Jojo. I nodded, not really wanting to know what that work had entailed, especially as he was famous for throwing junkies with debts through walls.

Not at them. THROUGH them.

'Stevie in?' I asked, hoping to talk to the man himself and avoid having to use the 'public' areas.

'Mmrrmm no... he back ten.' Jojo whispered in his odd groaning voice. Rumour had it that an opponent in the drug and gang trade had sent a man to kill Jojo, and he had even managed to slit Jojo's throat before he met with a particularly painful death. They said that Jojo had bent his spine backwards with his bare hands. He certainly had the scars, right over the voice box.

Another rumour however, blamed an equally dead ex-girlfriend. I just nodded in answer, idle chatter was wasted on Jojo. Instead, I headed straight for the oddly decorated waiting room Stevie kept, it's style reminiscent of a country cottage. I had no idea that drug dealers liked gingham and pine in combination.

It really wasn't worth going into the general public rooms. Despite the fact that his runners kept you in good supply, they couldn't give me anything near as good as what Stevie himself could for me. I plonked myself down and waited, feeling the remains of the last hit I took finally seep away into the floral abomination of a couch. My mind was now laid bare, idle thoughts and lack of a buffering high letting the painful memories filter back in.

My mother had been beautiful and was a rather famous faerie and model locally. My father had apparently been infatuated with her for a whole year before doing anything about it. She was kidnapped her one night, he had grabbed her after a night out on the town chased by the paparazzi. He was holding her captive in a dug-out basement he had custom made for the task.

He kept her imprisoned for months before she finally fought back and killed him. They found her stumbling through the streets, naked and bloody, heavy with child. She was desperately clutching a crude knife she had made by chipping stone from the slate floor. The months of torture and 'love' had driven her mad, after she had fought so hard for her freedom, they merely locked her up.

She gave birth strapped to a bed in a mental hospital. I was promptly sent into the state system, but my elderly paternal grandmother, feeling guilty about the evils of her son, had set up some kind of fund. I had at least gotten an excellent education, which was pretty rare in Bayton.

While said education meant I stood out from the average person here, it didn't protect me from the scum that clung to the area, infesting all aspects of life. I had learnt at the age of 13 that sex was an excellent currency and an even better weapon at times.

I shivered and rubbed my arms vigorously, trying to soothe away the memories of their prying eyes and bodies. Luckily for me, Stevie chose that moment to enter the room in grand form, throwing himself forward in that highly aggressive manner that all bad men bore. His short hair was buzz cut to his bony skull, the years of his life counted in both wrinkles and scars.

A fan of leathers, Stevie dressed all in black, but rather than being gothic it was just menacing. It made sense really, the worn leathers were testament to a life of actual suffering, rather than a fashion choice. Stab wounds healed to scars showed through the holes in the leather caused by the same knife. Painted on toughness was no match for the real thing, no matter how much eyeliner you wore.

'Jessie me lovely dame, 'ow is life for de prettiest of dem all?' he drawled, settling himself on the couch across from me, having to rearrange his myriad weapons to do so comfortably. I nodded at him, trying to not let my growing desperation show.

'I'm ok Stevie. Been an ok day for me so I thought I would drop in for a few hours and spend my pennies.' I was trying to keep it light-hearted for the sake of this ruse. I couldn't really tell if it was working or not, the fogginess of withdrawal having well settled in my brain, filling every crevice.

'Naw Jessie, ye stay here till mornin' eh? Gon' keep ye safe, eh?' Stevie looked so concerned that it actually registered through the fog. I tensed up. Perhaps he really did care. That was a scary thought to hit, even though I did kind of already know. Not just anyone could nap in his safe house or get far better stuff than they paid for.

Regardless I nodded rather happily, this little favour meant a night off the street, a good sleep and a good help to nod off. My heart would have leapt if it wasn't dead as a door nail. But far be it for me to whine about a broken heart when a good snooze was so tantalisingly close.

'Aww really Stevie? You're the greatest. Really means a lot.' I stopped myself before I blathered on too long. Fresh bullshit always stunk the worst.

'Naw, 's not nothing Jessie, but ye look like ye beat. Here ye take somma this 'n we get ye all rested up.' He threw me a little bag of pills, sweet, beautiful opiates to slow the incessant whirring of my mind. Knowing how good his personal stock would be, I opted for only one of the pale pink discs, settling it under my tongue and trying to ignore the bitter taste it left behind.

I thanked Stevie and motioned to throw the baggie back, but he waved them off.

'Naw Jessie, ye keep 'em. Reckon I got me sommat to talk about with ye when we ready. Got sommat I be needing sommen' smart on.' I nodded to Stevie, barely listening as every nerve in my body began to ooze liquid sedation.

I flopped back on the couch, utterly satisfied with my beautiful high, gazing up to the ceiling and letting myself float. I probably should point out at this point that no, faeries do not have wings. It would be wholly impractical. Butterfly wings are so delicate, and they would just be constantly ripped apart. Stupid idea! The high was working.

No, we are just children of nature, with most still living as close to her blissful embrace as possible. Those of us who live in the cities and are cut off, well, we find our bliss elsewhere. I had read somewhere once that pretty much all the city living faeries were addicts of some kind. Beauty and the beast alright.

While my mind wandered along these somewhat happier paths, Stevie had left me to immerse myself in the thick, oily doze of the opiate. I merged with the couch, feeling like I was being sucked into the centre of it, and yet at the same time I felt light as a feather. This is what I had craved, and I dozed off into sweet, blissful silence.

Chapter Two

S tevie gently woke me in the morning, well, afternoon with a steaming coffee and some kind of pastry. My stomach growled viciously but first I took my pills, not wanting to dilute them with food too much. As they started to settle in my blood, I wolfed down the free food with sips of scalding coffee. When he was content that I was settled and listening, Stevie began to elaborate on what he had alluded to the previous night.

'So, we got dis problem. Someone been messin' with de drugs we sellin'. 'Ts weird stuff Jessie, we thought they just high, but dey go real nuts,' Stevie said, rubbing a hand over his shaved head wearily. Wondering what he was on about, I just nodded, to get him to keep going so I could eat some more without having to speak. 'Dey messin' with de drugs, makin' dem users like a zombie, ain't respond to nothin'. Den dey just take off, ain't no one knowin' where. I gotta get ye help Jessie, ye smart, can go ask round and see what ye find? Mebbe askin' other dealers if it happenin' to dem? I ain't got de goods to go into dem's territ'ry yeh? But ye smart an' pretty, ye be ok to be askin' dem. And ye be faerie, can do all dat magickal bit. 'He was looking at me so earnestly, with so much expectation. It scared the life outta me. This sounded serious, like lives could depend on this... not exactly my forte.

'I dunno Stevie, sounds like some weird magickal shit going on here. Maybe we should get the Agency in.' I replied pretty lamely, almost muttering it. For good reason it turned out, as Stevie looked as if I had just slapped him across the face.

'Hel Jess, get sommat Agency people in, say em drugs gone magick. Yeah dat be good for business, done 'ave cops snoopin' an' me be locked on up. Can't trust em, ye I trust. Ye gotta help me, if ye do, I give ye food an' get ye room here yeh? Ye can have ye own room real safe. No streets for ye.' I am pretty sure my mouth dropped open in shock as he spoke. I hadn't had my own room... well ever really. It had always been dormitories or share rooms or the streets. The idea of it now boggled my mind.

Guess just asking around about these drugs couldn't be too bad. I found a way to rationalise it fast.

'Yeah, ok Stevie, deal. Will go ask around. Where did you want me to start?' Thanks to now having to be alert, I popped an upper to finish waking me up.

'Well, dere be Nathaniel over in North Bayton, he sellin' to all dem rich folks dere. Den deres Damien who in Bayton Central. But he run dat market at night yeh? Ain't gonna be out till den.' Stevie spoke of his fellow gang leaders thoughtfully, this time running his hand down his long goatee. I rummaged in my bag for my notebook, taking down the details of who and when just as the upper began to fizz through my bloodstream.

'Ok Stevie, I'm gonna get onto that then, go see... uhh... Nathaniel or whoever I can talk to. I'm guessing I shouldn't say you sent me?' I felt like being a bit cheeky. In the slums, just knowing the wrong person could get you killed. Stevie actually managed a smile.

'Dere I was thinking ye all smart and stuff. 'Fore ye go, Imma show ye the room I got for ye.' He stood up and waited for me to do the same before leading me out of the waiting room. We turned a series of corners, Stevie leading me into an area of his place I had never been to before.

He stopped at a fairly interesting door; spray painted with intricate silver spirals and patterns. He produced a key from his pocket and unlocked it with a great deal of awkward flair. The room inside was so simple but pretty, with purple and silver colours. It had a large bed and no windows, being in a safe house. It did however have another door, and I looked to Stevie questioningly. He just kind of smirked and jerked his head toward it, making me even more intrigued. I bounced over to it, expecting it to be locked for some reason. It creaked open to reveal something I hadn't seen in a long time. A bathroom, and it was private.

'You're gonna let me stay *here*?' I was afraid it was too good to be true. Stevie grinned from ear to ear.

'Yeh girly, thinkin' ye be enjoyin' this. If ye doin' my work I gotta keep ye safe. Clean 'd be nice too. Don' want ye stinkin' up me home an' all.' He laughed hard at that, but I was too buzzed to care. I was dying to jump in that shower, feel hot running water for the first time in years. Normally it was a cold bucket bath or hose down, depending on where I could find the water. He held out the door key to me and I practically floated across the room to get it. I undid the clasp on my most valuable possession, my silver necklace and jewelled locket and placed the key on the chain.

I thanked him profusely until he left, after which I really had to fight the urge to jump on the bed like mad. I locked the door for some privacy, another novelty, before jumping in the shower clothes and all. They sure needed a wash too, and Stevie had even provided some nice smelly soap which I made full use of. I left my jeans and t-shirt drying in the bathroom while I padded out to my room, wrapped in a fluffy towel and a state of bliss. The bed was screaming out for me, and I flopped down onto it, sinking into the thick covers.

I must have dozed off again despite the upper, because the next thing I remember was a splitting headache as the withdrawals brought me screaming back into the world. Groaning, I pulled my bag over to me, rifling through it until I could find my pillbox. Those lovely pinkies that I had been given last night would be too dozy to take now, so I grabbed some lower-level blues and an upper for good measure.

I did have to work for this lovely room after all.

My clothes were adequately dry that I could pull them on again, although the slightly damp and cold bra made me cringe. I dug through my bag for my make-up, ecstatic that I had a full mirror for once. Normally I had to use a broken chunk of mirror I had found in a bin. I applied my make-up quickly, with a much-practiced hand. I even combed out my bangs and gave my faerylocks a roll.

I smiled into the mirror, pretty impressed with the difference a shower and some effort made. It could also have had something to do with the fizz now running through my veins, making the whole world a bit sparkly and special. I pulled my worn boots on, followed by my jacket with the fluffy trim and I was ready to go. Looking down, I also lowered my shirt front and perked my boobs up a bit more, *a little extra help was always appreciated right?*

Chapter Three

The extra effort had helped me on the streets a little on my first fact finding adventure, but it didn't make an ounce of difference to Nathaniel. He had flounced into the tastefully decorated waiting room with a perfect smile and perfect clothes, right down to the perfect manicure. Stevie hadn't seen fit to inform me that Nathaniel was actually also a raging twink. He was followed by a huge man who was covered in tattoos and scars, a hulking mass of don't-fuck-with-me. He was apparently very well acquainted with Nathaniel, given that as soon as he sat down he was draped in a certain well-dressed twink.

'Scho,' Nathaniel began with the cutest lisp ever bestowed to a grown man. 'I haven't seen you here before, what brings you to my neck of the woods?' As he asked, he ran his fingers playfully through the man-mountain's hair. I tried not to smile at the lisp, especially given the angry stare of his thuggish boyfriend.

'Well, uhhh Nathaniel... I am here to see if there is weird stuff going on with your drugs too. I have spoken to Stevie from...' At that Nathaniel burst into laughter, stopping me dead in my tracks.

'Hahahaa, ahh Schtevie the Schouthie. Is the old fool still pretending he runs the South part of this Hel hole?' Nathaniel giggled loudly, even prompting a smile from the hulk. I ignored the jibe about the man who was now apparently my landlord.

'Yeah I guess so. Apparently, people have been using something and just kind of stopping? Then they take off or something.' I didn't want to give them too much information, just in case. Nathaniel cocked his head at her, finally losing his exaggerated cheer.

'Aye, I know something about it. Why is it that you care?' Despite the thick lisp, his direct nature stopped me in my tracks. He was clearly a canny man, and he wouldn't let much pass. I took a moment to weigh up my options and finally decided to just be straight despite my earlier resolutions. Lying messed with my high anyway.

'Stevie asked me to look into it, he is worried. I have an education, and he offered me a place to stay.'

'Ah I see. Well, as long as you keep your trap shut about anything you see in these walls, we won't have a problem. If Stevie suddenly starts sniffing around my get up here, I will come see you first remember.' Nathaniel nodded and tapped on the shoulder of his muscle. I nodded in reply, not really willing to incur his wrath.

'Asch it happens we are having a bit of trouble, so this could work. Some of my sellers in my rooms and on the street are telling me that we are having people going missing. They are taking this new shit, faerie fizzer and they just stop, standing up. First few times the drug was just a high, now it makes them freaks, they just walk away, and no one sees them again. Can't stop them either, they just keep walking,' Nathaniel said, sitting forward and finally focusing for once. I shivered a little, suddenly feeling cold despite the high. Perhaps it was wearing off too soon.

'So, has anyone tried to restrain them? And it's only this faerie fizzer yeah?' I wrote as I spoke, taking the time to fill out my notebook on this one. The irony of investigating a drug called Faerie Fizzer did not escape me.

'Yes and yes. The ones we keep a hold of just keep walking till they bleed or die. And the only ones affected, they take that faerie shit,' he answered snappily, seeming annoyed by something.

'Well sorry, I will try to work this out, so your customers are safe-'

'Hah! No, bad drugs means they take their money somewhere else. If they die or disappear, they ain't buying no more. Less sales to these addicted idiots.' The self-satisfied smirk on Nathaniel's face was suddenly itching for me to slap it off. The comments were hitting just a little too close to home. I thanked him and left, knowing I should ask more, especially about the supplier. I found myself not wanting to spend another minute around this man.

I walked out of North Bayton feeling pretty sorry for its residents. These people had the kind of life I had dreamed of. They had mortgages, jobs, a morning commute, stability. I told myself I was stuck in the gutter from all those rotten things happening to me and using the drugs to forget them. But these people I envied still had their own problems, and clearly their own addictions.

That reminded me to see to my own, and I did as I walked over to the central part of messy little Bayton. The market wasn't due to start for hours, but it would be good to scout out the area and see if there was any money to be made.

Odd jobs were good to find, and community notice boards were full of requests. In the past I had been a life art model, a dog groomer, even putting in shelving and picking fruit for one elderly couple. Most jobs relied on my looks, but at least I had found enough that I didn't have to take to the streets. That kind of sleaze could never be scrubbed off, even when I had the money after to pay for a place with a bathroom. When I had perfected my little hallucinatory act it made that work a lot easier at least.

Unfortunately for me there were no jobs posted, nor were there any desperate men seeking to lighten their cash load. Instead, I just had to wait.

Time passed quickly, night fell soon enough and Bayton Central came alive. I wove through the crowd, holding my bag tighter than ever to keep prying fingers out. My bag was all I had, it had my life in it, plus all the money and drugs I owned. The bodies around me pressed close, a general flow through the market kept people moving until they found a stall they liked the look of and dove in.

I went with them, in no rush to see this Damien. I hadn't just gone shopping in years, certainly not just wandering along and buying something that wasn't drugs. I tried not to wonder how it had come to that, distracting myself with some cute bone hair beads and colourful wraps. I was still picking through the stall when I was roughly tapped on the shoulder. It made me jump, so I turned around to give the tapper a piece of my mind. Too bad that said tapper turned out to be some seven-foot-tall block of thug.

'What do you want?' I spluttered, bravado being the best option here. Well... hopefully.

'Damien want to talk. You come now.' He had the usual neanderthal era speech capabilities that all hired muscle seemed to have. Considering I needed to talk to him anyway, I agreed to go without sass. I got the feeling I could either walk there or go unconscious and bleeding. Walking willingly seemed like a dandy idea to me.

'Lead the way, meaty boy!' I chirped, probably a bit too cheekily given the snarl he gave me, but the block turned and led as requested.

Chapter Four

Damien's rooms were surprisingly low key, lacking the usual pageantry of a local drug lord. I glanced into the rooms as I walked along an oddly plain hallway, no pictures broke the expanse of black painted walls. Each room seemed to be brightly coloured, glaring out into the monochrome hall. There were few people around, most keeping to the specialised rooms to fuel whatever habit they chose. As much as I couldn't, I desperately wanted to go in, "I'll have what she's having" and forget all about the zombie drugs. Nothing like a good long holiday from reality.

We stopped about halfway down the hall, entering a room that looked scarily like the waiting room at a doctor's office. Meaty jerked his thumb at the chairs before lumbering back down the hall. I took a seat, wondering why they were fine with just letting me run loose. A glance around the room gave me the answer.

Cameras peeked back, their unwavering gaze coming at me from every angle. I was betting there would be someone monitoring the receivers, who would mount a pretty swift response if needed. Vowing to be on my best behaviour, I shifted to get comfortable. Dealers tended to make you wait, leaving everything to their convenience to remind you of who was in charge here, so it was pretty surprising when a man entered the room barely a minute after Mr Meaty had left.

The solemn man was tall, well-muscled, very handsome in a scarred and rough way. He clearly favoured the current punkabilly trends, a tall but feral pompadour with skull tight shaved sides and rolled up jeans. His shirt was crinkled and hanging loose, while his jeans were stained and dusty. Dark circles encompassed his eyes, and his skin was pale, sickly. While he had the style, he looked a mess. Still, the man needed no protection, oozing an aura of bad-assery. As he sat down across from me, he looked me over suspiciously, something unreadable passing through his eyes.

'What'n Stevie be wantin' 'ere?' he asked frankly. I was almost surprised at how direct he was. Almost.

'Are you Damien?' I tried to dodge his question. I resisted the urge to ask how he knew I was sent from Stevie. Blunt is good, or blunt can get you killed. Pretty sure they didn't have narcotics in the afterlife.

'What of it?' The man responded, giving this conversation the intensity of a verbal ping pong championship. I decided that honesty was the best policy here too, without the bluntness.

'Well, I am looking into these weird occurrences around this one drug, I thought you might know something more. Stevie did kinda put me onto the case so to speak.'

'An' 'ow is it that ye talkin' so well, bein' another Baytie user?' Damien's suspicious glare bored into my eyes. Yikes, this guy did not like me, and he sure didn't trust me. I met the glare evenly, rising to the challenge without joining the pissing contest.

'I got an education. That's all. That's why else Stevie asked me to look into it.' I paused, still being looked over like a particularly disliked meal. His glare was beginning to piss me off now, gone way beyond rude and into utterly contemptible.

'So, yer just follerin' Stevie's orders eh? Ye ain't that fancy much.' The man was becoming snide to go with his asinine attitude.

'He first alerted me to the issue and set me on the- uh- case. However now I want to get it solved for the sake of all of us.' I delicately curated my response, feeling like I was tiptoeing through a minefield.

'Aye, so ye be some great saviour. A junkie Jesus come'n lead us all ter safety, eh?' The anger in me surged with each of his slurred but cutting words. The smell of booze stewed off him, enough to burn my nose. There was also the stench of unwashed man running under it all, and musk was not my thing.

This sulkiness wasn't getting me anywhere about the disappearances, and I had far better things to do than talk to this surly teenager in a gang banger's body. Like digging out my eyeballs with a rusty teaspoon.

'Fine, don't go too far out of your way to sort this crap out. I will just work with Stevie and Nathaniel. At least they give a damn about their own 'Baytie users' as you call them!' I stood to leave, ignoring the moment of wooziness in order to save face.

Turning to the door, I had only taken two steps before Damien was up and out of his seat, looming over me. To my own surprise, rather than being scared I was seeing red. The continued assholery was less intimidating and more an annoyance with every passing minute. He still didn't speak, so I stared him down before breaking the silence.

'What the fuck do you want now? I am leaving, I am getting out of your damn territory and be damned with your arrogance,' I raged as his dismissive attitude finally snapping the final connections to my patience. I flipped him the bird for good measure and stepped around him. The tantrum may not help my little investigation, but I felt a damn sight better. I felt him watch my every step towards the door, his gaze a prickle of awareness across my neck. He was measuring each step, sizing me up as I left. The second my toe touched the floor of the hallway, he inhaled sharply.

'Hey kid, sit'n down, I tell ye what ye want to know.' The second he called me kid I wanted to keep walking but knowing that there were people like me out there who were being abducted by this drug stopped me. I turned slowly and levelled my gaze at him.

'Well then, old man?' I shot back. His help may be very useful, but I couldn't resist the dig. Unexpectedly, Damien actually almost smiled.

'Aye, shut the door, sit'n down. Ye remind... yeah, I help ye.' He had been about to say something but had clearly nixed the idea. I trudged over to the empty seat that was closest to the door. Clearly Damien was either a thinker or a bit paranoid, all chairs stood with their backs to the wall and far enough apart that if someone attacked, there would be a good response time.

'Well, what of it?' I snapped, trying to keep my bluff going. Damien nodded slowly.

'Same as 'em others. Been seein' this drug come in, but I ain't seein' where from 'n how. Ain't none o' my regular guys got it. Thems hate it, an' know I got it banned. But t' ain't for naught. Keeps on comin' in. Dirty stuff.' His rough voice became reflective as the hostility left his words and posture.

'So, you don't know who is supplying or selling it?' I searched his body language for the truth. He didn't appear to lie when he answered bluntly.

'I ain't got the knowin' on it, and it got me fucked. No one sellin' an' yet it still gettin' in my territory, Hel, under my damn roof.'

'Under your roof? You mean it is even getting into your rooms here?' That part shocked me. Controlling the streets was one thing, but having this drug even sneak its way into the private rooms of the local leader was certainly something else. It was supposed to be almost impossible, as the private rooms were reserved for the best clients using the leader's own products. Somehow it was getting in, and people were using.

'Aye, it be happenin' here, and I ain't happy. Ain't be knowin' what ter do 'bout it, so iffen ye need help, I can give yer what ye need. It ain't right.' Damien scratched at the messy stubble of a beard, then appeared to look surprised by its existence. He tried to smooth it down, unsuccessfully.

'Any idea how many people have been affected?' I asked, taking note of the fact that Damien had become decidedly more accommodating. He nodded and pulled a notepad out of his back pocket.

'Aye, it been 34 people gone now. Tried to keep the first ones here, but they done snuck out. Even hit Luis. Can't stop em from goin' where they goin' so tried to follow em, but the ones I send to tail the junk-affected people, they ain't come back. Finally, just stopped tryin'. Lost too many men to it.' A twitch of his hand indicated that Luis was apparently Mr Meaty. I popped down all the information in my book, surprised to see the level of information Damien had on the Faerie Fizzer users. He clearly cared more than he let on.

'Got anything on the supplier at all?' I was hoping for a nice simple, straightforward lead. I could bust the supplier, he would be dead by sunset, and I could be nodding out for the evening.

'Nope. Can't catch anyone with it besides the users. They ain't talkin' either. Questioned 'em on who they got it from, and no one got any word to say on it. Hel, they ain't got any word to say on anythin'. I just, I don't know what to do.' Damien sighed as he ran his hands through his pompadour, pulling it out of shape. Perhaps this was why he looked so wretched. I nodded quietly, trying to decide on my next course of action.

He watched me carefully, making my skin itch. I never did like having attention on me, unlike my mother.

'Ok, well I guess that will have to do for now. Will try to talk to some of the users myself. Y'know, user to user.' I shot that jab out at Damien and must have hit a nerve, he had the grace to cringe.

'Aight, lemme know if ye be needin' anythin' else. Ye know where ter find me. An' make sure ye be telling me what be happenin' with what ye looking at. I got my interests too.' Damien stood up abruptly. He attempted to smooth out the crinkled shirt, brush off the jeans in some kind of impotent show of cleanliness. I just smiled politely and itched to leave. It wasn't his gaze, but more a general sense of unclean that made me feel like I needed a scalding bath. Finally, he pulled a dog-eared card out from his pocket.

'This is me phone number. If ye need anythin' ye be callin' me. Ye need to talk to anyone in my territory, lemme know.' He said as he handed me the grubby piece of card. It featured a Chinese dragon coiling around his name, Damien Niel.

'Oh, yeah I don't have a phone. Guess I can borrow Stevie's.' I replied, sure that Damien would be thrilled for Stevie to have him on speed dial. He grimaced but didn't say a word.

As he passed to open the door for me, I was again assaulted by the stench of booze and sweat. This man perspired whisky. The cheap stuff. I practically bolted from the room, muttering that I would interview the patrons another day. Trying not to run, I slammed the reinforced main door open and strode out into the sunset.

All things considered, I was pretty impressed with the progress I had made so far. I deserved a good high and a long sleep, but not before I washed the sense of cloying filth off my body. The walk back to Stevie's territory was a long one, so I had plenty of time to think.

The marvels of hot water and a good gooey opiate were multitudinous. My face felt caught in a smile a mile long as the steam plumed around me. The heat was easing the tension in my legs from all the walking, and I was truly grateful for the room. There was even a fluffy robe waiting for me to sink into. This was the kind of luxury I had only dreamed of, hot water, clothes that weren't threadbare, even a TV.

This was the kind of life I wanted, and every man I fucked, every grimy coin tossed to me after performing in an alleyway, it was all for this. I flopped down on the bed, letting my faerylocks slap down around me like a halo. They were chunky and twisted, the matted remains left after you didn't own a hair brush long enough.

When I had gotten in, I had full intentions of going over my notes and maybe interviewing the people currently indulging in a high. The rooms were only 20 paces away, but right now that seemed like an almighty chasm to traverse. My eyes burned as heavy lids slid over them and I was powerless to stop them.

'Guess Imma just rest my eyes a little.' My words were lost to an incoherent mumble as sweet unconsciousness took control.

Chapter Five

Daylight barely crept in past the heavy curtains, but it was still enough to throb around my head. I cursed myself, having slept so long I was now again withdrawing. My body wasn't used to the luxury of an undisturbed sleep in a soft bed. Groaning loudly as I blindly felt around for my bag made me feel slightly better, but relief only came when I found my little tin of pills.

Painfully slowly, the world around me normalised and I was able to stand. While I had been so distracted with the hot shower I had forgotten to wash my clothes. They were balled up on the bathroom floor, and I tried to freshen them up with a little bottle of perfume I had swiped from one of those big chain stores.

Pulling on the thin top and ripped jeans reminded me that I needed to get new ones soon. The holes were getting beyond what could be called fashion. Having a mirror was another luxury, and under the harsh lights of the room my clothes seemed even more shabby. I needed to go make some money, but I doubted Stevie would want me to bring my work home. I took out the last stub of an eyeliner pencil and quickly darkened my eyelids, mimicking the smoky eye the other girls usually favoured. When I was happy enough with my appearance, I packed up my bag and locked my room. The fact that I could actually lock a door for the first time in my life still gave me a fizz of excitement.

The walk to the central sex district was a short one, a region considered neutral territory for all involved. Every building had a red light, giving the whole region a red glow. Each of the boys in charge, Stevie, Nathaniel and Damien had their own facilities for their own areas, but none had ever managed to tie down the blocks that surrounded the Kulture Hole.

On the streets it was affectionately and aptly named the K-Hole. It ran under the guise of a nightclub, but most definitely landed closer to a brothel. Any woman could work there with relative safety after paying a door fee. I chose to work there on most nights when I could spring for the fee, as the clients couldn't rough you up. Sometimes they even bought you some drinks. Today I was skint though, so I had to work the roads around the K-Hole and hope I could lure someone wanting to pay up and no conversation.

Thanks to it still being daylight there were less girls out, but unfortunately there was also less clients. I trudged up the street, looking for a place to stand and look suitably alluring.

Various cars drove past until a man finally walked up. I barely registered his face as I muttered some kind of pseudo-seductive platitudes.

'How much?' he grunted. Good, I liked them dull.

'How much ya got?' I shot back, running a finger down his arm.

'Give ya $250. Full works. Mouth too.' He was resembling a grunting pig the more he talked.

'Cash up front, business is open. No kissing,' I replied firmly as I held out a hand while gesturing to the alley with the other. The man stuffed a small wad of notes into my hand and lurched towards the alley. I began carefully counting the money.

'No condom.' I grinned and followed behind him.

'As you wish.'

He leant against the heavily graffitied wall and began to unzip his pants, fumbling around inside. I gave him the heavy lidded, slow blinking kind of smile that men seemed to like and slunk over to him. Seductively I ran a finger up his naked arm, and I had his mind in seconds.

He began to moan, taking himself in hand and pumping away. I maintained my hold on his arm to keep the hallucination going while I leant on the wall myself. The surroundings were fairly uninteresting, a dusty utility alley for the various businesses in the area. Broken glass and fits littered the floor, and only colourful graffiti broke the monotony of concrete and asphalt.

Luckily a kind of dusky twilight had fallen, so we had a relative kind of privacy. He was really working himself up now, so I changed the fantasy accordingly. Idly I chewed a stubby nail, starting to get bored with how long this was taking. Normally the client would be halfway through orgasm by now. Not this guy. He was still moaning away; face flushed a scarlet red and sweat soaking his shirt. Time to get creative. I changed the hallucination again and he contorted, back arching and his free hand shaking wildly.

He came in a pathetic splat on the floor. Before I released him, I quickly cleaned up his hand with a tissue. I splashed a little water on my face from a bottle in my bag as an extra touch. When his senses returned, I was sweaty, breathing heavy and zipping my pants up with what I hoped approximated to a satisfied smile.

'Wow, no hook- I mean lady- has ever done that to me before. You are so worth it.' He enthusiastically praised me to the skies. I patted him on the back as I bid him farewell.

I took a moment to have a quick bump up before I returned to the road side. The sound of clapping made me jump in fear. Damien and Luis rounded the corner from the back of the K-Hole. I was amazed to see that he was clean shaven and polished up. The stench from yesterday was completely gone. Today he wore a red leather jacket, a freshly washed and pressed black shirt and some jeans she suspected were brand new. It was a stark contrast to her first impression.

'Ain't your territory, ain't ripping no one off, I swear,' I pleaded, preparing for a backhand. The money I had been given was already hidden away. Damien just laughed, looking oddly jovial for a man wearing an armoured leather jacket.

'Naw, Imma bein' impressed. Ye be pullin' some kind of magick on him?' He seemed genuine in his mirth. I was still wary.

'Sort of. It is a faery hallucination. We cannot make people do something against their will, but we can influence what they perceive. It is easier if that is something they really desire.' I was slowly backing up the alleyway towards the road so I could run if needed.

'Faery?' He asked with a surprised look on his face. The thought of having to explain it all made me groan aloud.

'Yeah there is a lot of critters out there. I am only part faery anyway.' As I spoke I noticed some sort of annoyance in Damien's stance when I mentioned critters. Interesting.

I was almost at the mouth of the alley now, and I had to lose Damien before I could get back to work. Having a well-muscled gang leader and his bodyguard hanging around would certainly be off-putting to any potential client.

'Naw, ain't a problem. I think it be real clever. Am impressed, and it looks like he got what he wanted.' Damien spoke low and quiet. I only half believed him.

'Well why are you stalking down back alleys?' I asked, hoping an awkward question might make him move on so I could get back to work. There was still enough night left to make another few hundred. Enough for some new boots and a good supply of Stevie's best. I had already forgotten that he had given me a whole bag full of pills.

'Looking at makin' a business deal. Thinkin' on buyin' the K-Hole, an' clean it up a little. Make'n sure dem girls looked after.' Damien whispered in hushed tones, as if he expected the competition to be eavesdropping on his plans. As much as what he said surprised me, I took it with a pinch of salt. Even if they started out with good intentions, it rarely lasted long. Either you exploit or be exploited in the Bayton gutter.

'Mmm-kay. Well, I have to get back to work.'

'Sure ye gotta do that? Ye wanna get somethin' to eat?' He seemed almost awkward, as if he were asking me on a formal date to a fancy restaurant.

'Uhh, no thanks. I have a lot to... do.' I finished lamely, not keen on elaborating. Damien looked a little disappointed but nodded anyway.

'A'ight, be seein' ye later. Come by my rooms when ye can, I got somethin' for ye,' he muttered as he gestured for Luis to follow.

I puzzled on his words as I waited for another client, shivering a little in the frigid city air. Despite the buildings being a windbreaker, all that concrete was freezing cold once the sun went downs for long enough. Even the thick layers of graffiti and posters could not battle the frost. It was a quiet night unfortunately, with few men trawling the streets with a pocket full of cash. When another few women surfaced on the other side of the road, I took my chance to continue my investigation.

'Hey, names Jessie. Just wanting to ask you some questions.' As soon as I spoke, they began to look at me suspiciously. The taller of the two spoke up after a pause just long enough to confirm that she did not trust me.

'A'ight. Am Liselle. This is Sadie. What ye wantin'. You ain't a cop.' As she spoke, she kept fluffing up her blue streaked hair, which strongly reminded me of clouds. It was clearly a statement, not a question.

'No, I ain't a cop. Do you know anything about a new drug called Faerie Fizzer?' With that, Liselle's face flushed an angry shade of red

'Oh, you thinkin' cos I'm workin' de streets Imma takin' em drugs eh? Ye jus' assuming I ain't got nothin' more than that eh? Imma workin' for me education. Gettin' em money cos I was real smart, just ain't had a chance fer school. Now ye be comin' and assumin' I ain't nothin' ain't ye? I ain't using.' With her final words Liselle spat aggressively on the pock-marked road. I had tried to intervene during her angry litany but had no success in the face of the onslaught.

'No, it wasn't that. I am investigating the drug because it seems to be adversely affecting the users. I was hoping you could help with information.' I tried to placate Liselle as best I could. Sadie continued to look up and down the street, seeming more interested in finding a client than anything I had to say.

'So ye are a cop?' Liselle squinted her eyes in suspicion. Her lips were pulled thin over her teeth in a sort of snarl, ready to tell me to get bent. For an older lady, she was pretty in a defiant way, her spine straight and shoulders held strong.

'No, Stevie asked me to look into it. People been having some bad troubles on it. No one knows where it's coming from. That's all. I just want it stopped.'

'Hmm. Well, I ain't got much on it, but Imma think Sadie might be knowing somethin'. She dealin' more with that than me.' Liselle stopped talking to tap Sadie on the arm. As she started speaking in sign language I realised that Sadie was deaf. In time Sadie nodded and signed back. 'She sayin' that she had a friend. He take em fizzer drugs an' jus' walked out. Ain't none seen him again. Been two weeks now. He done got em drugs in Nathaniel's lands. But she ain't know who from.' Liselle translated carefully. I nodded while I scribbled down my notes.

'Do you know his name?'

'Martine Maydwell. He never gone back to work neither. Was a chef at a cafe. Oh, a pastry chef! He been working at Maydwell's Urban Grind.' Responded Sadie, via Liselle. When I had copied all the information down, I thanked both women profusely for having helped me so.

'If you find out anything else, please let me know. I am staying in Stevie's rooms, The Fox Den. You know it?' Liselle nodded, an air of suspicion still tangible. 'Good. Leave a message there if I am not in and I will get it. Stevie really wants to get this sorted out, so he will make sure it's passed on. I will try to find Martine.' I spoke the last words to Sadie as Liselle translated. She nodded; her eyes frosted over with tears.

A true woman of the streets, not a single tear fell. Sadie was also defiant, but in a softer, rounder way. She had curves and skin like honey, sweet and golden. Her hair was clipped short to her head aside from a central fuzzy mohawk that was coloured with the fire of a dusk sun.

After I said goodbye, I decided to cut my losses and go home. I now had enough money to buy my way into the K-Hole tomorrow. Having a warm bed and a shower waiting for me cemented my decision. It was much easier justifying an early night when there was a home to go to. I trudged off through the icy scum while my mind drifted through the remains of my last upper. These missing people had to be going somewhere, and by the sounds of it, there had to be many of them.

This had been happening for at least two weeks. *How come I hadn't heard of anything until now?* I wasn't the most social addict, but surely someone should have offered me something by now. *Did they know?*

I shook my head vigorously, feeling far too illogically paranoid. There was no way they could have known I was working for Stevie in the last two weeks because I didn't even know that until two days ago. Two days ago, when I had to help find missing people. People who mattered, not like me. All I was good for was...

Sometimes I just didn't have the vim to fight that hateful little voice in my head, only enough to medicate it. I grabbed my beaten-up little stash tin for the necessary pep up to get me home. Luckily the streets were still fairly empty, so bumping up and negotiating my way back to Stevie's rooms was relatively easy. Once I had the door locked behind me, I finally started to relax.

A scalding hot shower and a whole lot of froufrou soap had me feeling more at ease in my own skin again. There was something about this little amateur investigation that already had me feeling jumpy. I would worry about a sleepless night, but that's what downers were made for.

Chapter Six

The day blasted its way into my skull the second I woke up. I had left my curtains open just a crack, but it was enough to obliterate any chance of falling asleep again. Some part of me had hoped that I would sleep the whole day away and then be unable to go to Damien as requested. I could reason that it was outside of business hours, knowing damn well that he did not run the typical business.

Alas, that illusion was destroyed. Sitting up made my head spin, so I lay back down and started searching for my pills. Luckily, I didn't have to get up to fetch my bag, habit from the streets dictating that I slept while curled around it. I popped the first pill under my tongue to let it hit my bloodstream fast, then swallowed a second. The pounding in my head became a sluggish throb, allowing me to slowly sit up.

Checking that my clothes were dry, I padded quietly into the bathroom to dress. I shaved the hair that was starting to grow out of my undercut with an old disposable razor I found in the trash one day, reminding myself to buy a new one now I had a little money and a roof over my head. This one was so blunt it mostly just tore the hairs out. Pulling out my eyeliner stub made me realise I also needed to replace that too. In the name of procrastination, I decided to go shopping before I went to Damien's.

Stevie would likely want an update too, which meant I would be even later. Anything to avoid that irritable alcoholic. Even Nathaniel was preferable to Damien.

Soon enough I was ready to go, my little notebook ready to inform Stevie of my progress. I still had to interview the people in the nod off rooms here, the modern-day opium dens. Still, I felt like I would be far too tempted to join in right now. The temptation would have to wait. I locked up my room and wandered towards Stevie's office. Loud wailing could be heard as I approached, someone with a voice already cracked and bruised from the effort. I loitered in the hallway, unsure of whether to interrupt whatever was going on. One of Stevie's assistants came running to the office, nodding to me on the way past. The frail young man entered the room without knocking, summoned by the intercom. Stevie's voice was low and inaudible, but I clearly heard the response.

'Jessie? Don't need to get her, she be inna hall there.' Said the assistant as I desperately tried to remember his name. Something starting with a G.

'Jessie? C'mere girl, be needin' yer.' Stevie sounded exhausted already despite it being only morning. I steeled my nerves and stepped over the threshold. Stevie and G-man as I was now calling him were joined by a nearly skeletal woman who was still sobbing into her grimy sleeve. Stevie was looking confused and saddened. His usual mask of indifference was down, his clothes crumpled and his hands shaking. Indicating towards the weeping, shuddering mess on the other side of his desk, Stevie quietly introduced her.

'Dis be my ex, Janey. She just got done tellin' me dat her brother gone and disappeared after him talkin' about tryin' some new drug. Dis time we gettin' lucky dough.' Janey wailed louder at the mention of getting lucky. I am sure from her perspective there was little luck in having a missing brother. 'He done gave Janey some o' the Fizzer stuff, 'n she brung it to us. Here.' Stevie passed over a dirty little baggie of pills. I hesitated to take it from his outstretched hand.

Even from this distance I could feel the sickly pulse of some powerful, sexual magick. Something slithered up my spine, twining around my throat. I felt scales rough against my skin. Fear chilled my bones. These were definitely not ordinary drugs. I should know.

The pills themselves were fairly nondescript. Pale yellow, and of course there had to be something glittery in it. They had a pearlescent sheen. I wasn't great with all the magickal stuff, but I could definitely sense that this had some kick.

'Well, there's something magickal going on, and I guess it isn't good.' I managed to stammer my way through the sentence. My mouth was dry; my hands itched from the power.

'You guess? You GUESS?' Janey became hysterically shrill at my timidity.

'I'm sorry, I am just really nervous! This is a lot of pressure. I know it isn't good, but I cannot track this kind of magick. Although...' I paused as I really focused down on the sensation of the magick. The resulting harmonisation distracted me completely from my train of thought. 'It's faerie magick. I can feel... but how did this happen? Faerie magick doesn't work when so detached. I don't understand.' My mind stalled. From everything I had ever come across the fae had to be in physical contact for their magick to work.

However here it was, running free in tablet form. Janey cleared her throat loudly. I could see why she was Stevie's ex-wife.

'This is something highly unusual. Something that shouldn't even be possible. This is a hypnotic style of magick that requires physical contact. I uhhh, have used it before.'

'So where is my brother?' she demanded, her green eyes narrowed to hateful slits. I felt as though I could choke on my own tongue. Her hair frizzed out with her anger, bringing to mind an angry street cat. The dirt smudging her face and melding with her tears completed the look.

'He can't be tracked from this. There is no trail as it is faerie magick.'

'Well get one o' them useless users from them rooms. Give 'em this an' make 'em useful. We can follow 'em,' snarled Janey, spit flying from her thin lips with every hard consonant. I instinctively leant back to avoid the spray, while desperately wishing I had some more narcotics on board before talking to this woman. My mellow was well and truly burnt away.

'But you might hurt them! Or kill them!'

'Who cares 'bout some junkie if it be gettin' my brother back. He matters at least.' She screamed now, loudly enough that my ears rang. I was stunned into complete silence. My mind desperately tried to grab at thoughts as they whizzed past, but nothing stuck. There was just no answer there. Stevie slammed his hand down on the table, making Janey jump and turn on him.

'No! We ain't gonna be sacrificing no one. We ain't animals. Dem people out there pay your ali-mony see? Dey ain't nothin'. Dey all be some folks brother an' sister see? We ain't gonna do nothin' like dat.' He spoke low and firm, shutting Janey down before she could get a word in. The shrew sniffled back her angry sobs before snatching her handbag off the table and stalking out. Stevie sighed and indicated for Jojo to ensure that Janey left the building.

'Dat bitch ain't never change. She always boostin' herself up on someone else's back. Sorry Jessie, ye know I care about ye all, ye ain't nothin' to me.' Stevie's sad eyes rolled over the room before settling on me. He was a good type, despite the kind of world we live in. My hands shook as I fumbled for my pill box, desperately trying to pull out some of my last sweet little opiates. Stevie nodded and opened his desk drawer.

'Got ya covered. Dis be clean as can be for ye, no nasty surprises. Here.'

The bag was full of the prettiest pills I had ever seen. I moved to grab a few out, and shoved my cash on the table, but Stevie stopped me. 'Naw Jessie. You take 'em. I be making sure ye be takin' the good stuff, all them be tested. Ye can keep ye money too. Make sure ye put it to good use. Really need ye to keep on dis. I... we be losin' more people every day.' I gulped, both from nervousness from the choking responsibility on me, and from being handed at least $500 worth of Stevie's top shelf offerings. My voice croaked when I tried to speak.

'Are, are you sure about this?'

'Yeah Jess, ye keep 'em. What ye off ter next?' he asked, gently prompting me for an update. I nodded as I swallowed a pill.

'Well, I talked to two ladies yesterday, and they know someone affected. He is missing too. Going to go talk to his workplace, maybe see his home. The women's names are Sadie and Liselle. Told them to get me here if they need me. I hope that's ok?' I paused, confirming with Stevie that I had done the right thing. A quick nod was all I needed. 'Then I was thinking to visit the rooms in someone else's territory. Thought they might recognise me here, especially because I have been staying here. Although not sure which would be worse, Nathaniel or Damien.'

I gave a twisted smile, equally perturbed by either. I also conveniently left out that Damien had asked me to visit, so I didn't have to explain where I had seen him or why he was there. While he didn't explicitly say it, my violent history had taught me not to spill the beans when a gang lord was doing something.

'Aye, both be real u-nique folks. Damien used to be a real good kinda man, but he got his heart broke. Some witch were takin' him an' leadin' him on, but then she done somethin' real bad to him. Now he ain't no good. Real sad, we used to compete but be friends. Nathaniel, we ain't never been friends. He only ever servin' ter look after hisself. But I be trusting ye ter be knowin' what ter do.' Stevie said by way of salutation. With that, the awkward little meeting was over, and I scuttled out of the den.

Chapter Seven

As luck would have it, Maydwell's Urban Grind was in the same area as some of the more reasonably priced department stores in Bayton. That cash was burning a hole in my pocket, and I was in dire need of some new clothes. Soon they would no longer allow me entry into the K-Hole. It may not be the finest establishment, but you still had to be relatively neat and, more to the point, alluring.

The walk over there was wet and miserable. Rain flooded the holes in my shoes until they became a squelching mess. When I finally made it to the threshold of Maydwell's I was shivering uncontrollably. As soon as the heavy door was pushed open, I was bathed in heat, with such a cosy and inviting aura that I felt unwelcome. Everything was a warm pine and gold tones, with accents of pumpkin orange in tasteful spaces. There were more cushions than I could count with blankets draped across every plush couch. It terrified me.

Nervously I approached the counter. I was expecting to be thrown out at any moment. The barista glanced over at me then paused. In my mind I rehearsed the argument to be allowed to interview them about Martine before they demanded I leave their nice little café.

'Hi, can I help you with anything?' she asked, as warm and friendly as the cafe itself. For a moment I was stunned, not used to politeness in such situations.

'I, um, yes. I was hoping to talk to someone about Martine Maydwell? I am investigating...' I could no longer continue as the pretty lady before me abruptly broke down in sobs. Alarmed, I looked around, but there was no one else in the shop. Eventually she drew in a deep breath and indicated to a nearby booth seat.

'Go sit down. I will make us a coffee and tell you everything.' She croaked out the words in a tortured, wet whisper, turning to the machines. I quickly sat down, keen to have a warm drink in this weather. While she crafted the drinks, I gazed around at the warm décor, opting for blissfully cosy rather than sterile industrial.

The barista reflected this, her warm personality reflected in her appearance, with warm Autumn colours present in her clothes. They complemented her dark skin, and this was about the point that she noticed I was staring, so I quickly began to inspect the table carefully.

The woman dropped off two coffees, and I eagerly piled sugar into it, warming my frigid hands on the mug. She returned soon after with a plate of warm scones with jam and cream on the side. My eyes grew wide at the aroma of food I usually only dreamed of. Still, I was hesitant to take one until the barista gave her express permission. I piled my chosen scone high with toppings before biting down with sheer joy.

'My name is Martina Maydwell. My parents thought it was funny to name their twins thus. Great joke.' Martina smiled, the false grimace people do when they are desperately unhappy. She sighed and continued. 'Martine is my twin brother, and we have always been together. We even went into business together when Martine graduated culinary school with a love of pastry. But he had problems. Our childhood was great up until high school. We were black, in an all-white school, in a white neighbourhood. Martine was never into sports, preferring home ec classes and the like. People just hated that we were different, but more so because they assumed he was gay. Martine was bullied constantly, then his grades dropped out completely. After that he became depressed and attempted to...' Martine stopped, choking on her tears and devoid of voice. I waited quietly, unsure of what to do.

Taking advantage of the heat, I surreptitiously slipped my shoes off under the table in an effort to dry my socks. If Martina noticed, she was kind enough to not mention it. Eventually she calmed down again as I stuffed down another scone. For her sake.

'Martine was given pain medication afterwards, but he was so depressed. He just kept taking it. Then he moved onto other things when they stopped prescribing it to him. He still graduated culinary school and still worked well here. But he took drugs to stay awake and focus, then drugs to sleep. Drugs to avoid the feelings, then more to feel again. I tried to help, and he went to counselling. He was doing better. Somehow, he got some new drug. It changed him over a day, then he disappeared. He won't answer his phone, I know he isn't at home. He didn't even take anything important with him, even his wallet is still there. You said you are investigating something?' Martine asked as her voice rasped to a stop again. It sounded like she needed to change the subject before she collapsed again. I obliged.

'Yeah, Stevie, a uhhh local leader, asked me to look into the disappearances in the area. He was concerned about the people in his, uhh, community going missing. Thought they might be related. Sadie passed on the details of Martine's disappearance to me.' I explained, while desperately trying to sugarcoat the situation.

'Oh, Sadie. Martine used to give free coffee and sandwiches to the local homeless people. She came in one day with a few of the others. He seemed to take a real shine to her, despite the difficulty communicating. She was lovely. Saw her waiting around the cafe to see if Martine was back every day. Pretty sure it wasn't for the sandwiches. I think they used together though. Call it twin's intuition.' Martina stared off into the ether, looking vague as she sipped her coffee. I finished a massive mouthful of scone before opening my mouth to speak. Martina beat me to it. 'See what I don't understand is that, if they were using together, why didn't she get affected, if it is some drug? Why did Martine disappear? Why is Sadie still here?'

Revelation bloomed in my mind. The shrew's missing loved one had also been male. I would have to see what gender all of the others had been, but a pattern was slowly trickling into daylight.

'I think you have a very good point there. There may be something in it, but I will have to check with Sadie to confirmed she used it too. How did Martine act before he left?' I was hoping to gain some insight in what the drugs actually did.

'Well at first it was just his usual self. I didn't even notice that anything was different. He seemed a little restless, but he usually is when he... he indulges. Normally he just cooks up a storm with all that energy, and we try whatever creation he has come up with before he wanders off for a snooze. This time he just had no motivation in the same way. There were orders to be made here, the last stragglers of the day. He just left a pan on the stove full of custard and walked out. Luckily the other cook spotted it before it started smoking too badly. When a half an hour passed without him returning, I knew something was wrong.' Her voice rasped to a halt, so Martina paused to take a long sip of coffee and a bite to eat. I simply basked in the warmth that was starting to settle upon me now that my socks were beginning to dry out.

After clearing her throat, Martina began to speak again.

'When we closed down for the day, I went home to see if he had crashed out somewhere. We only live around the corner you see. I just... he was not there. The last time I saw him I was furious that he would leave with customers still waiting. I just was so annoyed. When I asked around, a few people saw him leave and just start walking south. I tried to follow, and over the next week I walked up and down almost every street, scanned every face. My brother is gone. I know he is still alive, but no one has seen him in so long. I just don't know what to do.' Tears were beginning to stream down Martina's face as she gave in to wretched sobs again.

I was useless at comforting people, but I grabbed a napkin and offered it to her. It was hard to imagine what she could possibly be going through, but the opiates formed a nice buffer between me and any overwhelming emotions. I fancied that I looked rather professional right now and tried to display a suitably sympathetic but detached facade. Not that I did not honestly feel sorry for this woman, but I needed to look the part.

Still, I was beginning to overthink things again, so my last dose must be running low. A painful silence had settled over us while I dithered and Martina sobbed.

'Uh so he left on foot, going in a southerly direction. Do you know if he has accessed his bank accounts or anything?' I was trying to think of what the police or Agency may ask, feeling like a complete impostor all the while.

'Oh, I haven't checked. We do have a joint bank account to make it easier to pay ourselves from the business though. Let me check.' Martina fell silent as she picked up her phone and tapped away. I muttered a quiet agreement while swiping the last scone.

'No, it hasn't been touched. That is so weird for him. He usually spends a small fortune on the most trivial things every week.' Martina sighed and placed her phone on the table.

'Do you think he might have a separate, hidden account?'

'Hah! My brother abhors paperwork and distrusts banks; it is highly unlikely.' This time I got to witness a watery smile from Martina. She was so pretty and made me feel awkward while in the presence of her innate grace and beauty.

'So, uh, he hasn't used his accounts and no one else has then. But you are sure he is alive. Someone has to at least have him and is looking after him enough that he is still going. I know of other men having disappeared also. Maybe they are... well I cannot be guessing too much. If you don't mind, can I come in later in the week in case he comes back, or you think of anything?' I felt kind of oddly shy about asking, an unusual feeling like a rock in my stomach.

Maybe I had missed my last dose by too long, that had to be the reason. Martina smiled gently as she nodded. Once again, the feeling of being an impostor tore through my core, a pathetic addict pretending to know how to help this tall, curvaceous woman before me. Hel, it wasn't even like me to think about whether a woman was curvaceous or not. As I wallowed in my confusion, Martina spoke up, her tears finally slowing.

'Yes of course. Please, come and eat here any time you need. Anything to help you find him. I will keep note of anything I notice for you. Thank you so much for caring about my brother. I will have to thank Sadie too, for bringing it to your attention. We have no parents any more. I thought we were all alone in this, the police and the Agency didn't care at all when I contacted them. Acted like there was so much more important than the life of my brother. So, thank you.' She spoke so earnestly, pulling a trembling hand through her thickly curled hair. Her soulful brown eyes were sad but determined, and I really felt an admiration for such a woman.

Again, my stomach twisted as a fluttery feeling ran through me. I took the chance to jam my boots on and jump up while throwing on my bag. Unsure whether to help her carry the dishes away I stood there awkwardly holding my hands out. To my absolute surprise she took them in hers as she looked deep into my eyes.

'Honestly, thank you. I feel so much better knowing that you care. I am so glad that there is a private investigator on the case!' she exclaimed enthusiastically.

'Oh, I am not... going to let you down,' I responded, not wanting to dash this beautiful woman's hopes by revealing that I was just some street trash employed by her dealer. I could not do that to her last sliver of hope, despite the guilt of the lie. I bid her farewell and sorrowfully stepped out of the nice warm cafe into the street. Thankfully my socks had dried a good deal, and the rain had eased off.

The shopping centre was only a short walk away, and soon I was browsing the many different styles and designs on offer. I had never had a chance to follow any kind of fashion, usually it was a matter of what I could afford with the pittance of left over cash after buying my weekly opiate rations. Now I had actual money.

The shop assistants curled their lips and made sly derogatory comments, but I ignored them. It was a reaction I was all too familiar with. Still, the sneaky dose I had indulged in on the walk over here was softening everybody's rough edges.

Excited for some new boots without holes, I trotted to the shoe section. There were so many colours, so many pretty styles. I couldn't help but try some of them on. High heels, strappy sandals, glittery boots, I loved them all. Unfortunately, the streets were cruel to such pretty things. Instead, I settled on a plain pair of black boots, durable, practical things. Sensible. It left a bland taste in my mouth. Still, it meant no more personal puddles and muddy socks.

Carefully counting out what I had left, I decided that I could even get a new pair of jeans. My glee overflowed when I found a beautiful pair of black denim jeans that made me feel good about myself. They were even on sale, allowing me to get a few black t-shirts. While the sales assistants still sneered and carped on at me, they fell into stunned silence when I pulled out my earnings to pay the bill.

Suddenly they were all peaches and cream, smiling wide as the hundred-dollar bills were handed over. I wanted to spit on their pretty polished bench-top but instead was forced to give them a simpering smile and thank them for their magnanimous hospitality.

I clutched my bag of treasures tight, changing out my shoes and socks on a bench in front of the store. The old ones went straight into a nearby bin, and my warm toes inspired a sigh of happiness. This was the closest I have ever gotten to having an income which allowed for luxuries of this manner. The buzz of a full belly and new clothes died down a little when I remembered that I was supposed to see Damien, a guilty reminder fluttering through my mind like a moth with torn wings.

As an extra dose of procrastination, I resolved to find a public bathroom in order to change my clothes. I deluded myself into thinking that new, neat clothes would help me get up the confidence to talk to the man who made it clear that I held about the same value as street grime.

Still, Damien had requested my presence, and if it helped my little investigation I was obliged to attend. The door to his rooms loomed before me as I nervously waited for it to be answered. He must have allowed some local street artist to do a piece on the door, as it now sported a fierce red Chinese dragon, likely a nod to Damien's mixed heritage. Secretly I approved, always pleased to see new art breaking the dull monotony of Bayton's lower socio-economic regions. It gave a vague sense of cheer and hope to such blandly urban places. No one bothered to commission art in these streets.

While I pondered the new art I spaced out, so much so that I didn't respond when the door was opened. Sneaking an extra dose of opiates on the way over was probably a bad idea, given that the doorman was now giving me a vigorous shake while muttering about dozy druggies. Still, it snapped me out of it.

'I... I am Jessie. Damien asked me to visit. Gotta see Damien.' I muttered through the cotton wool feeling in my mouth. This was probably making a terrible impression. Damn that man for making me so nervous I had dosed a little too strongly.

'Jessie ye say? Mmm I will check. Stay here,' commanded the beefy door man, his face a mess of scars and mutilated tattoos. He pulled the door closed behind him again, and I gazed down at my numb feet, amused as I wriggled my toes in the new boots. By the time the slab of muscle returned I was rocking back and forth, feeling the spring of the soles gleefully. Beefy did not seem impressed.

'C'mon,' he snapped as he pulled the door open barely enough to allow me entry. It forced me to press against him to gain access. Whether it was supposed to be sexual or intimidating, I had no idea. As I passed him my nose instinctively wrinkled at the powerful stench of body odour and cheap cologne. Luckily, I had enough of a hold on my faculties to not stick out my tongue or gag aggressively. He gestured down the hall, this time pushing me past the little waiting room I had been in previously.

Marching me all the way to the end of the hall, he gently knocked on the door there. The shock at such an overly muscular, slashed up example of man-mountainhood producing such a delicate tapping nearly knocked me off my new boots. A laugh boiled up inside of me and spilled out before I could stifle it. In response, I received a glare, however I was saved by the door being thrown open and Damien beckoning me in. I happily acquiesced, keen to be away from a pissed off thug who probably just thought his manhood was being questioned.

As Damien took his seat behind a solid wooden table, I sank gratefully into the chair across from him. Everything in this office was black leather and a deep red wood I had never seen before. I was more surprised to see Damien all cleaned up, even more so than the last time we met. A black silk shirt with black jeans and creepers had him looking neat and dapper yet still retaining that slightly feral aura. Even in my new clothes I now felt under-dressed.

'Thanks, fer comin' Jessie. I was wonderin' if ye had much progress with dem drugs we all got problems with,' Damien asked, even opening up a notebook and fetching a pen to take notes.

'Uh yeah. I found two more people who have disappeared shortly after taking the drug. They just walk off. Oh, I am not completely sure, but I think it might only affect men. Do you know who has disappeared in this area?' I was hoping that a direct question would ease the intense feelings of discomfort.

'Aye, all been men, so far 's I know. Ye think there is somethin' in that?' His eyes were intense in their focus as he watched me.

'Well, there could be. A man will be far more susceptible to female faery magic if he is that way inclined.' I mused, thinking about the dynamics there. It could be magick specific for males, or just magick that would work on personal attraction towards the caster. There was little doubt in my mind that it was a female faery creating the magick in these drugs. Of course, there was also the drugs themselves. 'Has anyone tested what exactly is in the faerie fizzer? Not just the active component, but anything else that they may have mixed in?'

'None from my folks. Ain't easy to find it. It even bein' in my rooms, but I ain't able to find it.' Damien began stroking his chin in deep thought. The effect was interesting given that he now had no beard.

'You mentioned before that it had gotten into your rooms, but how do you know it has if you can't find it?' I hoped I wasn't being too sassy, but my curiousity was killing me.

'Well, because 'em men be suddenly walkin' out, ain't collect their stuff or nothin'. Just walkin' away out th' door.' I was frankly shocked about how congenial and open the man was being. Based on my first impression I had thought that he was barely a step above a feral beastie.

'I don't suppose you know which direction they took when they left?' I was feeling hopeful, but given Damien's earlier recalcitrance towards drug users, I hardly expected him to care which way they went.

'Aye, every one of 'em went South-aways. We gone and followed 'em but always be losin' 'em. I feel like some'un be helpin' 'em disappear. Cos my men, dey good, you know, smart men. But each time, dey lose 'em.' Damien nodded as he spoke, clearly frustrated. It almost sounded like he cared again, I was further surprised by this strange man. I decided that bravado and humour would be the best mask to wear right now, things were getting too congenial.

'Careful, it almost sounds like you care about those 'Baytie users' you are talking about.' Gosh it was petty, but I couldn't help the little dig at Damien. He actually winced as if in pain.

'Aye, I be sorry fer that one. Ain't like that. I jus' fergot meself... fer a while. I do be carin' even lost a man I considered me friend. It were wrong fer me to be sayin' that, especially to ye.' As he spoke, he was looking at me oddly. Damien seemed truly contrite, which took me by surprise. He had been so negative, so angry. I had thought him incapable of such emotion and empathy.

'Er, yes. So, if that is all you wanted, I thought I would just hang around in one of your rooms and see if I can notice anyone doing anything of interest to the, uh, case.' I muttered, feeling flushed.

'Oh yes there is somethin'.' Damien handed me a sleek black box. 'Be noticin' ye ain't got a phone. Keep ye safe. Don't wanna be callin' Stevie.' Now it was Damien's turn to fall into awkward muttering. The box did indeed contain a phone, one of the latest smart phones with all the fancy attachments. They cost more than I could ever consider.

I was speechless. My mind had stalled completely.

'I got ye credit too, so ye don't have to be payin' fer no calls or nothin' fer a while. This is my number, ye can call me whenever ye needin' me.' Damien handed me a slip of paper with his personal mobile number on it. Just like the man now, it was clean, unlike the barely readable card he had given me last time I was here.

I nodded numbly, unable to formulate the words to thank him, tell him it was too extravagant or bless his entire family line. No one had given me a gift such as this since I had escaped my grandmother's clutches. I nodded again, willing moisture into my mouth, which had decided to mimic a desert.

'I... thank you. This... I can't take such a gift. It must have cost you so much. I can never repay you,' I pleaded to deaf ears.

'Ah nonsense. Don't want no payment. Want to be keepin' ye safe,' Damien replied, quickly standing in an attempt to hide the blush I saw creeping into his cheeks. I was so confused by all of this. Previously Damien had acted like he abhorred my entire existence, and now he was all gifts and blushes? Stuffing the box into my bag, I muttered another pithy platitude and bade a hasty retreat to the rooms.

Chapter Eight

The rooms attached to the Central den were simple and clean, a testament to their quality. I went to the counter to buy an hours' worth of opium-based entertainment but was discreetly waved away. Apparently, Damien had already talked to the dealer and was prepared to foot the bill for my little charade. I settled into an inconspicuous corner, ensuring I could see the entire room. An attendant soon brought over a loaded pipe, as was the tradition for such rooms.

There were also various pills available, but I needed a nice big show of just being another user. Sneaking in a quick upper to prevent dozing off during the day, I began to slowly draw from the pipe as my eyes wandered the room.

There were a few patrons lying around in various stages of inebriation, all oblivious to my gaze. No one appeared to be interacting with anyone apart from the dealer. Damien had reassured me that there was no way his approved dealers would ever pass faerie fizzer, so I was sure it must be passed between people in the rooms somehow. I sat and smoked for an hour, relighting and drawing away the last of the pipe. While people came and went, no one seemed to do anything out of the ordinary, nor did anyone approach me.

Eventually I gave up on this little fishing expedition, stretching slowly in my velvet lined world. As I arched my back to loosen the muscles that had grown weary in my poorly seated daze, one of the male patrons noticed me. As I walked past to leave, the ugly oaf actually grunted at me!

'Eh, you got tricks? Working? How much?' His voice was thin and slurred with opiates and spittle, but I got his gist. I quickly summed him up, noticing an over filled pipe, extra pills and expensive clothing.

'$350, full service,' I replied curtly. He looked mildly surprised; well, I only assume he was surprised as his eyebrows slowly lifted.

'Pricey bitch. Better be worth it. Outside,' He snapped, beckoning an assistant to protect his precious pipe. The thought crossed my mind that Damien probably wouldn't like me pinching off some income, but it seemed like this guy had plenty. For $350, I was willing to take the risk and possibly incur a little wrath.

As soon as we were alone, I entranced him, barely willing to touch him, let alone get intimate with his sweaty, corpulent flesh. The opiates running through his system made him incredibly pliable, but also hard to gain and keep an erection. I had to get highly creative to get the cretin to blow. At least I was left with a happy customer and $350 of unexpected cash. I carefully stuffed it into my bra, unwilling to lose so much money by accident or misadventure. At this rate I was actually gaining some sort of financial stability.

The fluffy haze of warmth from the session in the rooms coddled me back to my own room at Stevie's place, leaving the streets in soft focus and muted colours. Laying down on my bed to have a nap, I fished out my newly made money and counted it again. With what was left after my shopping spree, I still almost had $400. This gave me a slow rolling giggle. How preposterous, me with money. Clutching it to me like a teddy bear, I slowly dozed off in the wide bed.

Coming to in the evening was tough. My mouth was dry, with a feeling like I had been sucking on chalk. My pulse flared at my temples and caused me to groan loudly. After a few seconds I realised that the pulse wasn't only in my head, but someone was banging on my door in the real world.

'Minute. Just... minute.' I tried to shout, but instead only managed to produce a sad croak. The hammering continued. I dragged my corpse out of bed begrudgingly.

The creak of the door was enough to make the pain in my head flare viciously. Jojo stood there, his face flushed with exertion.

'Aye, Jessie. Been got another one. Just up and ran off from the rooms. Been chasin' him.' He toned in that unusual whispery voice.

'When did that happen? Where did he go?' I demanded, finally feeling more communicative due to the urgency of the situation.

'Bout ten minutes ago. Chased him all the way up to th' corner o' Damien's land. But got blocked off, an' he gone. Left all his stuff here.' Jojo puffed out, finally starting to catch his breath. I nodded and left my door open while I went to grab my bag. I knew my room was safe with that hulking mass of meat by the door. I surreptitiously slipped my money back into my bra as I popped a few pills into my mouth to deal with the pain currently drilling aggressively into my skull.

Locking the door behind me, I followed Jojo to the third of Stevie's rooms, notably far from the main door, which suggested someone reasonably well acquainted with the venue. Sweet smelling smoke filled my senses for the second time that day. My mind fluttered with excitement at the threat of more indulgence, but I had a duty to try and find this missing man.

I was directed to the man's possessions, spilled out over one of the low-lying tables. Taking the wallet in hand, I quickly checked the ID, so I knew who to look for. The victim appeared to be a rather burly type, bald headed, a large, crooked nose and reddish beard. Mr Adam Rogers was confirmed to be the one we were looking for by Jojo, so I quickly memorised every detail I could, including the fact that he had even left his shoes behind. I opened my senses up to detect any faery magick present and quickly detected both a trail and a stray pill on the floor. No one else in the room had any traces present.

'Hey Jojo, did you notice anyone leave after this guy?' I was forced to snap, pressed for time as the trail was dissipating.

'Hmmnnnn no Jess. Been chasin' that man ove' de town. Ain't seen no one leave. Ain't knowin', eh?' He shook his head slowly as he responded.

'OK, I will get after this trail, there is definitely something fae about all this. Grab that!' I shouted and pointed at the pill as I headed for the door, surprising a young woman dozing in the corner. I quickly apologised for startling her and ran for the streets.

The trail was still easy to determine, being sickly sweet and pulsing through the twists and turns. It wove in a serpentine, slithering back and forth through every greasy alley and crowded street. Every now and then a man would walk through the magickal miasma and would stop still. This magick clearly had the ability to entrance others simply by proximity to the afflicted person.

Still, it didn't seem to have full hold, as they mostly continued on their way between pulses. A few even needed to be pushed out of my way, standing slack jawed and staring in the middle of the street. Once free of the trail, they were back to normal. This felt like whoever was behind it was amping up their power,

I was beginning to tire by the time I made it through town. The trail was dissipating and had curled into a more industrial area. Due to the evening rapidly falling to darkness, I became acutely aware of the potential for danger here. Still, I had enough courage to continue on. Given my street smarts, I figured I could deal with whatever came at me. I wound through the various warehouses and wholesale store fronts, but the trail abruptly disappeared.

This area seemed to be a warren of streets and alleys, and my breadcrumbs were gone. Turning this way and that, I took out my pills with hands shaking from exertion. I had no real idea of which way to go, and I could only assume the reason the trail stopped was because Adam had made it to wherever he was being pulled to. That meant wherever it was, it was at least a 20-minute walk from where I was. Sighing, I popped my pills away and started to walk back.

I was almost clear of the industrial zone when I heard heavy dragging footsteps behind me. The stench of stale alcohol, piss and sweat overtook my senses as I whipped around to face the person behind me. He stood, swaying, an obese parody of a man. Balding, his greasy face was obscured by thick glasses and dishevelled facial hair. The booze made his skin ruddy and sweat acrid. Carefully taking a few steps back, I assessed my options. When he spoke, it was barely comprehensible through the spittle flying freely from slack lips.

'How haff yeh be here? Yeh wanna go yeh lookin' fer sommat ter do? I gotya.' He lurched forwards as he grabbed his own crotch. I leapt back a few more steps, unwilling to turn my back to him and run. 'C'mere yeh tease. Yeh be out onna night fer this. Don't be runnin'' when yeh know yeh want it.' With that he ran at me with surprising speed for someone who was so drunk he could barely stand.

I yelped as his slimy hand wrapped around my wrist, but this was the opportunity I needed. Reaching out etherically, I trapped his mind. I carefully created an alternate memory, removing myself and simply having him fall down and knock himself out. For an added touch, and my own revenge, I punched him square between his glazed, bloodshot eyes. He dropped like a rock as I released his mind.

Running the rest of the way back to Stevie's rooms had me gasping for air like an asthmatic, but the adrenaline kept me going. When I wheezed my way up to the door, Jojo looked at me in surprise.

'Ye OK Jessie? Ye lookin' like ye been seein' somethin' bad. Ye found 'em who takin' the men?' His voice sounded even more odd, as he was trying to speak in a hushed tone. That unusual wheeze sounded more like a stiff breeze in a forest. Swishy. I tried not to hyper-focus on his odd voice in my adrenaline and opiate coated haze. I needed to hear the words.

'Yea- no, I didn't find them, but I have a better idea of location. The trail cut off when... I need a map of Bayton if you have one?'

'Hmmm no Jessie, I be havin' one fer ye tomorrow. That be okay?' he answered, nodding in recognition of someone walking by.

'That will be great, thank you.' I answered, gladly going inside to my room. It seemed that the streets were a little unfriendly tonight.

Still the worry that I was getting too used to living in such comfort sat impatiently in the back of my mind. *How could I go back to roughing it after this?*

If I solved whatever this is, I had no doubt that Stevie would have me out before long. He was a business man after all. These were the thoughts crowding my brain as I lay on the bed, begging for sleep to take me from this fear.

My woes seemed to invade my sleep, and I was caught in a dream within a dream. There were horrifically mutilated bodies, men screaming for my help and loathsome arms grabbing at me in a perverse manner. When these night terrors finally subsided, I was plagued by visions of duality, night and day, light and dark. Two pieces fitting together to make a whole, completing a cycle, turning a wheel. It was these images that burned into my psyche as I awoke with Martina Maydwell's name on my lips. Could there be something in the fact she was a twin? I lurched out of bed in excitement.

Chapter Nine

Quickly showering and throwing on my new clothes, I wondered where I might be able to get information about twin links. There was a single run-down library in Bayton Central, wedged up against the cemetery and assorted other public amenities buildings. The night market run by Damien would also have a collection of various magickal folk that I may be able to glean some greater information from as a backup. Forgetting all about eating, I grabbed my bag, threw some pills in my mouth and practically ran out of the door.

Hesitating at the crossroads, I decided to go suggest my idea to Martina first, eager to see her again. As I strolled over to the cafe, I was surprised by a loud beeping sound. Looking around, there was no one there, and yet the beep sounded close. Suddenly I remembered the phone I had been given. Opening my bag, I found the blaring, flashing thing and answered the call.

'Hello, um this is Jessie?' I felt unsure of how to greet people on the phone.

'Aye, it's Damien. I gotta get ye to come down here. Got a dead body. Looks like one of 'em involved in all this. Can ye come to me rooms?' Stress had ragged Damien's voice, and I actually began to believe he did care.

'Oh no. That's... Is he... how?' I answered weakly.

'Lookin' bad. He real skinny, real bruised. All pale too.'

'Pale? So he isn't black?' I asked with a spark of hope that at least it might not be Martine Maydwell. It felt callous to the dead man, but I couldn't help it.

'Naw he white. Red hair.' Damien answered my questions with a curious note to his tone. I ignored it.

'Okay, I have to go somewhere now, but I can come by after. Is the body... still where it was?' I tried once again to think of what a real investigator would say, feeling like a big fake.

'Yeah, we just cover 'em up. Thinkin' ye want to see it first. Got me a guard on it, makin' sure no one mess with it. Good yeah?' Damien's voice was full of uncertainly, just like mine.

'I guess. I mean that is good, please leave it like that.' The effort to sound professional was heavy on my mind. I was uncomfortable with so many people thinking I could possibly have any authority or help anyone for that matter.

'Ok, well ye can come to me rooms when ye can, and Imma take ye to the place of the body. Jus' be lettin' me know when ye be on yer way. Sendin' me a message.' Damien chose his words very carefully, seeming distracted by someone nearby.

'Uh, yeah, I will. Right.' I muttered. Rather than attempt any kind of pithy salutation, I simply hung up. Shortly after I remembered to save Damien's number so I wouldn't be surprised again, only to find it already in the system. How had I not noticed? Technology like this always frustrated me.

Feeling all jumbled up, I popped an extra pill out of my pillbox, taking down some of these irritating jitters. Normally I wouldn't do so in the middle of the road, it was just asking for trouble.

Still, desperate times called for desperate measures, and just a little faerie magick. All around me felt a glow of euphoria, cutting off any nefarious ideas. Hard to mug the punky kid who clearly has drugs when you feel that life is dandy right now. Leaving a small cluster of dazed but happy people, I hastened over to Maydwell's Urban Grind.

Before I entered the cheery space, I self-consciously checked my appearance in the reflective office windows nearby. My hair had been growing out and became less scruffy thanks to the various hair products and regular bathing. The new clothes even made me feel good. Overall, the woman in the reflection looked much healthier than I was used to. It actually shocked me a little.

Entering Maydwell's elicited the same mouth-watering response as last time. The smell of roasted coffee beans and baked goods were intoxicating. There was a decent line of people in store today, so I joined the queue. The young woman taking the orders was unfamiliar to me and unfortunately Martina was nowhere to be seen. As nervous as I was, I still needed to talk to Martina herself. The line of famished customers was whittled down until it was my turn. In an uncanny moment of serendipity, Martina Maydwell managed to burst in the front door, puffing as she carried armfuls of grocery bags in.

As she lugged her bounty through the occupied tables, I caught her eye and gave a dorky wave. Internally cringing, I simply smiled as best I could when she noticed who it was.

'Jessie, good to see you, please come with me, we can talk in the kitchen while I unpack.' She spoke with her sunshine and honey grin. Today she had her hair out natural, the tight curls making a halo around her head. Gold themed make up only enhanced her beauty, and I felt like a giant gawky fake as I clumsily bumped my way through every table to follow her. Pushing my way through the saloon doors, I came face to face with both Martina and another woman, this time an older black lady.

'Oh, is this your mother?' I asked carefully. Martina and the woman burst into peals of laughter. My heart fell through the floor as the urge to vomit rose. No amount of drugs could have prepared me for this interaction. Why was I feeling so weird?

'Oh hell no honey. My momma is dead, remember? Janelle is a good friend of mine and is an excellent cook. She came in to help my other cook when Martine disappeared. But you can trust her, she cares for him all the same.' Martine gave a gentle giggle as she dropped the bags onto a cleared counter. Janelle nodded her head curtly and turned back to her sizzling grill. Burger patties and bacon left an amazing scent on the air. My stomach gave a traitorous growl which I quickly tried to stifle. Martine disappeared into the massive walk-in refrigerator with one if her bags.

'Give 'em fries a shake up for me, girl.' Janelle ordered gently as she quickly flipped the patties and grabbed down plates. I had never done food service in my life, but I found the deep fryer and pulled up the basket, shaking it gently. 'Naw girl, give it some grease!' She shouted, without a hint of anger. I shook them far more vigorously and re-submerged them.

Within seconds there were buns on the plates, salad flying everywhere and patties coming off the grill.

'Ok girl, pull up 'em fries and hang 'em on that wire like the other basket.' I quietly obeyed while sauce bottles were being flung around and brandished like weapons. She gestured for me to fill a bowl with the fries. Simply lifting the basket was a struggle, but eventually I managed to tip them in. Salt was flung in, fries tossed and portioned onto plates as Janelle rang the service bell loudly. I stood in awe as the most mouth-watering food was now being taken away by the tiny waif of a waiter. He looked like a delicate elf yet still managed to carry 5 plates at once. Janelle quickly turned back to her grill and threw on yet more patties.

'Get 'em more fries from the fridge eh?' She muttered as she pointed towards the door with her spatula. I couldn't avoid grinning at the casual way she had dragged me into forced labour here, not that I minded. Anything to help Martina. I pushed my bag onto an empty shelf and trotted over to the fridge. When I got inside Martina laughed heartily at my request, showing me where the bags of fries were.

'I will be out in a minute, then we can talk. Sorry about this Jessie. We are so short-handed without Martine.' I tried to mutter some response about how I was happy to help or the like, but apparently my mouth decided it was again time to imitate the Sahara Desert.

Clutching the bag of fries, I nodded awkwardly the whole way back into the kitchen.

When the next lot of fries were on and Janelle had me cutting open burger buns, Martina finally emerged from the refrigerator. Her eyes were reddened and perfect make up now smudged. Opening my mouth to ask her if she was OK only served to get me quickly interrupted.

'So Jessie, do you have news for me?' Her voice cracked and hands tremored.

'Yes, I... well sort of. I have a better idea of where these men are going now. I was wondering if we could use the link you have with your brother to narrow down his location further. I need to do some more research first, but we might be uniquely lucky that you two are twins.' I answered as I shook the fries and was directed to fetch some plates as well as take away wrappings. Once again condiments and toppings were caught up in this whirlwind of a dance by Janelle.

'That is good, but what is the bad news you aren't telling me?' The question was shrewd. This woman could read me far too easily.

'There is bad news. The first body has shown up that might be a part of the case. I don't know for sure yet, I need to go to it after I am finished here. It's not Martine though.' I added in quickly.

'Oh I know Martine is still alive, I do know that much. I still feel him. But this news scares me. He feels exhausted.' Martina's voice almost exploded into a sob, but she held off her tears.

I was struck again by her control and dignity. This glorious woman had her world falling apart around her yet still kept up a near perfect facade. I checked and drained the fries as Janelle put the finishing touches on the burgers. Martina unpacked more of the groceries as she spoke.

'I will go over immediately to investigate this... body. Then I can research the twin thing. Oh! I have a mobile phone number now too. Erm. You can contact me... on it. If you want. Need!' Oh, I was being a dope again. I turned back to my fries and threw them into the bowl.

My face felt like it was exploding with a brilliant redness. How did professional people handle this? I had never been a professional in any legitimate field before.

Working the streets didn't count, the closest I had was working in the K-Hole. I was too caught up in my anxiety wallowing to notice that Martina had approached me. Of course, that then made me jump when startled.

'Here, my business card. Text me your details when you can.' She gave me a watery smile, still stunning despite the tears bordering her dark eyes. I nodded dumbly as I shoved the card into a pocket. Janelle finished up plating her latest creations and rang the service bell impatiently. As the plates were being collected, I said my goodbyes to both women. After wrapping the takeaway order, Janelle stuffed it in a bag and passed it to me.

'Who is it for?' I asked, looking out of the saloon doors to see who was waiting.

'Eh, it be yours. I heard that stomach going.' In her coarse, husky way, Janelle was so sweet. Now it was my turn to start the waterworks.

'Are you sure? I can pay,' I asked as the tears stung my dry eyes. Janelle simply snorted and went back to wrangling her grill. I looked at Martina.

'Consider it a part payment for helping out and finding my brother. We both need that right now.' As Martina spoke she nodded towards Janelle. I inhaled the intense aroma of the food I had longed for so. Giving a teary nod, I made my exit to squirrel away my food.

That burger was every bit as delicious as I imagined, with a variety of spices, sauces and fresh salad. This was the kind of food I had not had the luxury of eating since I went on the streets. Even the fries were a sensation, made with actual potatoes, spices and just enough salt. Even with, or perhaps because of the dead body awaiting me, I took the time to sit and eat on a bench seat.

This fancier part of town even had a little green park, with children running around and lovers taking picnics. While I may have looked a little wistful at those happy, loved up faces, it was not the life for me.

At times it felt as though I didn't even know how to have an emotional connection with someone in that way. In the past, having an emotional connection to someone in my life had proven wounding, if not deadly. I had more of an emotional connection to these heavenly fries.

Then a mischievous little intrusive thought popped into my head, nebulously suggesting an emotional connection to Martina. The blush tore up my neck and face as I jammed every last morsel into my mouth so fast that I almost choked. Stomping off to escape my own embarrassment, the park was suddenly less cute. In fact, it was loud, bright and awful. There were smug people flaunting their loved-up relationships. I could feel their judging eyes on me as I left. I now hated parks.

My foul mood made the walk to Central Bayton much faster than I had expected. Standing outside the door to Damien's rooms as I desperately tried to catch my breath, I remembered that I had wanted to question some of the more magickal stall holders at the markets. The temptation was overwhelming. I could either go check out a dead body with a man who despised me but acted oddly, or chat about fascinating links between twins. I dithered on the doorstep, knowing which one I preferred, but also which one was more of an urgent nature. A dead body lying in the street would attract both attention and pestilence. Before I could steel myself, the door burst open, narrowly missing me as I jumped back.

'Jessie, ye be here. We best be goin'. Me man I got watchin' the body ain't none too happy 'bout it. He been callin' and textin'. C'mon girl.' Damien grabbed my hand as the door slammed closed, apparently prepared to manually drag me to the body if needed.

'How did you?' I asked, looking at the faces around me.

'Eh, there be security cam'ras see?' He pointed hurriedly to the multitude of security cameras bristling from every angle.

Of course. He still tugged at my hand, so I couldn't help but follow.

'How far is it?' I didn't want to whine, but I was feeling short of breath again already.

'Not far. Don't need to drive.' He responded as he pushed his way through the crowd. Two meaty security guards fell in with us and would clearly be joining us on this jaunt.

'Do you recognise him?' My voice came out annoyingly breathy. *Why did such a voice always sound so sexual?*

'Naw, ain't seen him here never. He real skinny, ain't got tattoos or nothin' I can see. Nothin' really obvious anyways.' The path was a winding one through some alleys, although I could tell that we were heading in the same direction as the trail I had followed previously.

Damien retained his death grip on my hand until we stood before a thick crowd of people. Now I realised why we had two massive guards. They simply parted the grumbling crowd with their meaty arms, although few were ready to complain when they saw that it was Damien coming through. These people seemed to genuinely like him, even smiling and nodding a greeting as they were pushed out of the way. I was surprised, but that was short lived when I saw the body.

Chapter Ten

Living on the streets of Bayton meant that I had seen plenty of bodies before, from overdoses to murder. This body was different. This body *felt* different. He was absolutely skeletal and appeared twisted. His spine was bent oddly, fingers gnarled and some were clearly broken many times over. Bruises littered his entire body, and he was lying out on his back. Much of the skin on his right side was an odd shade. It was as if he had a body wide bruise, although there were large pale patches within it. Something about this triggered a memory, but I couldn't place it.

Reaching for my notebook, I remembered that I now owned a phone which was capable of taking pictures. My hand brushed my pill tin as I rummaged through my bag. I desperately wished that I had taken a much higher dose. A little numbness right now would have worked wonders. Finally, I found my phone in a far-off crevice in my behemoth of a bag. I began to snap pictures and take notes but was distracted by the goofy smile on Damien's face when he saw the phone. I chose to ignore it.

There were odd welts on the man's back, which reminded me of whip marks. The man was skinny, but also surprisingly muscular. I was no expert, but this seemed unusual. It was almost as if the man had lost all fat, however had worked out aggressively. Muscle, sinew and bone all stuck out at odd angles. This man had clearly been over worked and under nourished.

\Wherever this man had been, he had been treated like a slave, with little healthcare. Flies were already gathering around the body, so I looked him over as quickly as possible. There was very little in the way of identifying features. He was even shaved completely bald, with only red eyebrows a visible indicator of what was.

He was dressed only in a pair of plain shorts, and his feet were heavily callused and cracked. This man had either never been a fan of closed shoes or had been doing some intense work without them. This seemed to be as much information as I could glean out of the body, so I started to look at the surrounding street.

Unfortunately there was absolutely nothing unique present, this was a well-used alley with much of the standard city detritus. Discarded paper, flyers for gigs, needles, chewing gum, nothing out of the ordinary.

There was nothing else to be done bar the one important step that I dreaded to do above all others. I placed my bare hand on the corpse. My senses flooded, the smell of dirt and blood, digging, a meal of thin porridge. The same faerie magick bound all of these memories together, a pink haze. This man was definitely connected to my case; however, it was impossible to make out any details from this poor husk. I walked back to Damien.

'Ok well, I guess I have done everything I can do. Short of an autopsy, there isn't much more information that can be gleaned from this poor bastard.' I tried to keep my voice low, to cover my contempt at the images and impressions I had seen. The gathered crowd were already curious enough.

'Well, I be thinkin' I be knowin' a doctor might help us. She doin' all the surgeries and stitchin' up of the folks round here. She always helped those on the streets and all. I'm thinkin' she may be helpin' us again, to be savin' more people. I will get this body wrapped up and packed away and ask her help,' He finished, motioning to the gathered guards. They produced a tarpaulin and quickly rolled the body securely in it. They quickly moved off with the body held between them, the two burly guards effortlessly carrying what was now a frail husk of a man.

'You think she would do something like an autopsy though? Not many people would want to deal with... inhumanity.' I asked carefully, trying to phrase it as delicately as possible. Damien just shrugged as the crowd dispersed before offering me a cigarette. I nodded more out of politeness, as I had my own. He lit both before passing one across.

'Can only be askin'. She a real smart doctor, ain't like she wouldn't be knowin' more about that fella's inner workin's. Gimme a minute.' Damien stepped a few feet away to be polite but remained within earshot.

'Hey Doc Celeste. No, no, I am fine, and me boys. No, but we do got a problem. There been that new drug that be makin' them folks disappear yeah? Well, I found me a private investigator for it...' I tried not to snort with laughter or derision. He had been so recalcitrant at the beginning, but phrased it as his own idea to bring me in. As it was I had to stifle a smirk but forced my face to neutral before listening in again. '... Ye be a normal doc and all. But we got a dead man, and this Jessie be sayin' she need an autopsy for her case. No, you know 'em Agency or police don't be comin' here. They ain't want none of this. No, ain't no one gonna look but us. OK, I will take it there. Thank you. I appreciate it.' Damien hung up and turned back to me.

'She good?' I knew the answer but wanted details.

'Yeah, she said she got a friend in West Bayton who got a vet surgery. We take him in, and she will come and do as good as she can. Ain't no guarantees, but she got some testing and things she can do. Apparently it's all the same for 'em animals? I dunno.' He looked a little confused at that, but Damien certainly could bring people together. I had to hand it to him; he was far more involved in this than Stevie or Nathaniel. Perhaps my early impressions were wrong, and the real man was the one all his people seemed to love. Or perhaps it was just because he had finally taken a shower and shaved.

'OK, so we have an autopsy. That's... great. I guess. Soooo, when is it?' I was hoping I would not have to attend. Unfortunately, I didn't really trust anyone else to take good enough notes for me.

'Aye, gotta be after they close. So be around 6:30 tonight. That gonna fit around your... work?' he asked gently, and I was astonished to see no hint of derision.

'Well, yeah. I was hoping to get over to the K-Hole tonight, but I can do it after. You still gonna buy-' I was shushed quickly by Damien placing a hand over my mouth, surprisingly gently.

'Aye, we don't be talking like that now eh?' He asked, rather than threatened. I could have kicked myself for my faux pas. Of course, he didn't want me blabbing his business plans to anyone around. I felt like a fool. There was a dead body in the middle of Bayton, of course there was a crowd.

'Yes. So, I guess I can get the address off you? Will walk over there in a bit.'

'Nah, I can be taking ye there if ye want me to grab ye. Be drivin' there anyway. You let me know, sendin' me a message and address beforehand yeah?' He didn't really wait for an answer before loping away. It was almost as if this big, tough man got shy whenever he asked me to contact him. Whatever, he might be nicer now, but he sure wasn't Martina Maydwell.

With that intrusive thought I blushed furiously, it was my turn to lope away feeling foolish.

Did I really like her that much? Was this even remotely professional?
Oh dear.

Chapter Eleven

As promised I messaged Damien the address to be picked up, about a block away from where I was really staying. He probably already knew where I was shacked up, but there was no need to rub it in. Nor to bring Stevie and Damien in that kind of close proximity.

I kept my notebook close and took enough pills to soften the shock of my first autopsy. There was no way I had ever expected to be doing this in life. Knowing I would likely head across to the K-Hole afterwards, I quickly slapped on some make up and cleaned myself up a little. It was not exactly a classy establishment, but I would have far more competition. Plus, I was in such a good place, it felt nice to dress up a little.

When all I had to look forward to at the end of the night was an opium softened nap in a dirty gutter, there seemed little reason to look particularly good. It wasn't like the clients cared anyway. But with a little extra effort at the K-Hole, I could land a better quality of client and make some better money while I was at it.

A glance in the mirror confirmed that I had pulled off something of a look, a little less fatigue and street grime. Close enough was good enough under "sultry" lighting. I took an extra bump for good luck and headed out. The various body guards stomping around the rooms nodded at me as I passed. Never before had I had such unfettered access. It was almost a sense of respect.

That was a worry.

Trotting over to the street that I had agreed to meet Damien on; I was glad that I had the foresight to do one far from Stevie's HQ. The streets felt uneasy tonight, tension clung to dark crevices and hushed tones. There was little I could do, and I was not in any kind of danger from the unsettled people keeping to the shadows. This felt turf related, and I made a mental note to ask Jojo about what he had heard from the whispers of the night.

Right on time, Damien pulled up in the street, nodding at me as I jumped in to the front passenger seat. I was surprised that he drove himself. Stevie never did, relying on the greater safety that the rear seats offered. Drivers were far more expendable to Stevie. Still, it looked like a nice car, for all that I knew about cars.

As we drove I felt vaguely uncomfortable in the relative silence. There was some kind of music playing, something I didn't know but it had macabre lyrics and a nice beat. Even that didn't help shift my jitters. I fidgeted nervously, the bump making me incessantly wriggly in an awkward environment.

'So ummm, the rest of your day go ok?' As soon as it came out of my mouth I cringed outwardly when I realised how domestic that sounded.

'Oh, uh, aye. It be good enough. Ye be lookin' good tonight.' He muttered as he stared resolutely out the windscreen.

'Ah, thank you. I thought that with going to the K-Hole, gotta look a bit nicer.'

'Aye, be lookin' to clean that place up some. Get 'em better security, nicer rooms. Security gettin' beat. Been girls gettin' roughed up an' infected there lately. Found that out from some of my girls. They been worrying about 'em friends.'

This took me by surprise. How did the man go from 'Baytie users' to caring about the safety of his sex workers and bouncers? Which one was really him? The two characters seemed like opposite ends of the spectrum. For the second time today, I was questioning the quality of the man I should be most wary of. He had previously mentioned something about testing his girls, but I hadn't thought him serious.

I sat quietly as I thought of something to say, noting that we had entered West Bayton. There was actually plants here.

'Well, I haven't been there too much lately, so it will be interesting to see. I guess it is still better than working the streets at least.' I mentally weighed up my options as I spoke.

'Eh, ye be careful then,' Damien replied as he pulled into the parking lot of a rather stylish veterinary hospital. Everything was stainless steel and art deco. I knew this was a richer area, but this felt utterly foreign. We walked in, and I was relieved to see that the waiting room was empty.

For some reason I didn't want to be seen while on my way to this clandestine autopsy. We were ushered in by a veterinary nurse who regarded us very carefully. It was clear she did not trust us in the slightest. Upon entering the room, she guided us to, a young woman and a slightly older man looked up. Before them lay the body of the man. I shuddered in response to seeing this poor meat sack again.

'Doc Celeste, I be thankin' ye fer this. Ain't no way we know who this is or what he been killed with. Be wanting to get him looked at. This here be the lady who investigating all that been going on, Jessie.' With that he turned to me. 'Doc Celeste be the one who patch us up and help when the Agency or normie cops don't wanna be bothered.' Damien fell silent, clearly as much of as explanation as I was going to receive.

Dr Celeste flashed a genuine smile, and I instantly felt a sense of trust toward her. She definitely had some faerie blood amongst her ancestors. The kind of glamour she exuded fit her role as a doctor perfectly.

'Damien, Jessie, this is Dr Brogan. He is the lead veterinarian here; however, he also has a background in microbiology and molecular genetics. That will certainly aid our mission for tonight.' Dr Brogan smiled wearily. Clearly he had been seconded to the cause after a long day. Still, his grey eyes were congenial. It was clear he bore us no ill will for impinging on his time. I simply nodded in response and pulled out my notebook.

Dr Celeste handed each of us plastic aprons and face shields. Realising how messy this could turn out to be, I stripped off my jacket. When the jacket and my bag were safely closed in a nearby cupboard, we began. Turning his limbs this way and that, the two doctors pored over the victim.

'Subject features marked emaciation. Extensive lividity to right hand side. Subject is a white male, blue eyes and bald head. Little bruising to his face, however it appears that two teeth, a canine and a premolar, have been knocked out or removed forcibly on his upper right side. Errr, hand me that torch please?' Dr Celeste asked Dr Brogan quietly as she forced the victim's jaw open. They conferred quietly before she began her dictation again. 'Dentition is degraded with multiple cavities, consistent with living in lower socioeconomic conditions. No dental work done from what I can see.'

Dr Brogan pointed at something on the left shoulder, then spoke with a surprisingly deep voice for such a slender man.

'There appears to be an injection site here on the upper portion of the arm. Intramuscular. Seems very recent, could even be around the time of death. Could be cause of death.' He spoke slowly and carefully. Dr Celeste nodded in agreement before continuing her analysis.

'Two fingers visibly broken on the right hand, one dislocated on the left. Significant bruising to upper torso. Feels like there could be some broken ribs under the bruising on the left-hand side. Are you getting all of this OK? I can go slower if you need?' Dr Celeste asked me kindly, with no hint of derision in her voice. I shook my head, keeping my notes short but useful.

'No, I can keep up fine. Thank you for checking though,' I responded politely.

'OK continuing with the external observations. Abdominal area feels sunken due to emaciation. Skin is all intact, but significant bruising to the left side, extending to the middle. Genitalia appears normal. Legs show bruising, especially around the left ankle. Possibly a result of a shackle or tether of some kind? It doesn't have any specific pattern or binding marks unfortunately, but that could mean he was fettered long term. Three broken toes on the right-hand side, none visible on the left. OK, turn him over.' Dr Celeste and Dr Brogan struggled to turn over this awkward mess of skin and bones.

The rest of the external examination had little more to offer, so the doctors agreed to get some x-rays before opening him up. I was glad for the warning ahead of time and snuck to my bag for a softening dose of opiates. When I looked up, I saw Damien staring at me, his face a mask of forced neutrality. I very specifically ignored it. I checked my phone while I was at it and saw that barely 30 minutes had passed since we started. It felt like far longer. I tried not to groan loudly as the doctors returned with the body.

'OK, it should just take about 10 minutes to get the digital results of the x-ray onto the computer here. In the meantime, I guess we better start on the, uhhh, internal parts.' Dr Brogan clearly was not a fan of doing so. I thoroughly agreed.

'Yes, pass over the surgical kit please,' requested Dr Celeste as she pulled on a second pair of gloves. Beginning with the classical Y incision I had always seen depicted in the few TV shows I had seen, the internal organs were slowly revealed.

My initial repulsion was rapidly replaced by curiousity. This was thanks, in large part, due to the bubble wrap now embracing my mind, but also due to my early fascination with all things true crime. I was taken back to the days when I would read books on the subject, or sneak into dorm's common room late at night to watch the TV. There was a hint of nostalgia for a more innocent time before the streets, sex and drugs, but I quickly shook it off. Now was definitely not the time. Nor ever, to live on regrets.

'Liver is enlarged and appears... wrong. Can you get something for me to put a biopsy in? It may just be fatty due to the starvation, but I want to make sure. Stomach has no contents, but bowels do contain matter. He was eating something at least, but not much. Internal reproductive organs all appear normal, as does the bladder.' The computer beeped quietly, and Dr Brogan moved to check it. He started poring over the x-rays as Dr Celeste continued.

'Moving up. Ribs are definitely broken, with cracks on many others. Suggests an extensive beating around the torso, possibly long term. Lungs appear good enough, although he was definitely a long-term smoker. Heart is slightly enlarged. No traumatic injury.' Dr Celeste stopped abruptly as Dr Brogan swore loudly. All of us looked at him in shock. He seemed too well mannered and quiet spoken to be cursing quite so much.

'That is certainly an injection site on the arm there. They did it so badly the needle is broken off in the arm still. It's just awful. Aside from that, there appears to be many broken or fractured bones that have recently healed. Some parts even have loose shards of bone around a healed area. Even his skull is fractured, along with the zygomatic arches and orbital bones. This is awful.' He was repeating himself in his shock.

'What does that mean?' I broke the awkward silence that had fallen while we processed what we had just been told. Dr Celeste answered instead.

'It means that he was routinely abused, then allowed to heal, then abused again,' she said grimly. 'An incredible beating, repeatedly, or something of equal brutality. Most of it fairly recent.'

I felt nauseous and rubbed my arms in some kind of soothing effort. If this man had been so badly damaged, what did that mean for Martine? Would he even still be alive?

Dr Celeste took various tissue and fluid samples. They were carefully labelled and placed in a fridge that would keep them fresh for the laboratory scientist to process in the morning. They seemed to be finishing up, with no more alarming observations to be made.

Glad to be done with this personal hell, I carefully finished my notes and went to return the book to my bag. My hands were shaking so badly that I could barely undo the closures. Quickly I drew out my hidden stash tin and selected some nice calming opiates. I mentally measured out the amount needed, given I had only dosed three quarters of an hour ago. I also had to be careful that I wasn't too docile at the K-Hole tonight. Business was hard to do when you kept nodding off. I looked up as I threw the pills into my mouth, washing them down with a sip of water.

Damien was staring at me with a look of concern this time. The look unsettled me. I don't know why, but I was compelled to stick my tongue out at him like a bratty child. He snorted, with either laughter or derision, I couldn't tell.

'Well, that concludes our work here tonight. Those samples will be prepped for analysis tomorrow; however, all the results will be available in around a week. We are lucky that this clinic has an on-site laboratory. Now are we finished?' The Doctor was clearly done for the night, but her annoyance seemed as if was not directed at me or Damien. After seeing the mess of a human we were investigating, I felt more like it was frustration at the loss of life, and in such a horrific way. I nodded and looked at Damien. He also nodded and stepped closer to Dr Celeste.

Muttered words were exchanged and accompanied by furtive glances. I idly wondered what their relationship was. It was clearly intimate, but without a sexual spark... or perhaps that was the ooze of the opiates talking.

I fiddled with my bag until Damien and Dr Celeste had finished talking, while Dr Brogan looked on awkwardly. The deceased man still lay in our midst, and I vaguely wondered what would happen to him. Caught up pondering my options, I didn't notice Damien approach until he stood before me, clearing his throat.

'Ahhh-errrr, we all fixed now?' I asked through a mouth that felt dry and full of desert dust it seemed.

'Yeah, be lookin' like it. Ye say ye workin' the K-Hole tonight? I can drive ye there, got some business need doing,' Damien muttered as he strode towards the door. Clearly I was expected to follow, a fact that I resented. It had been threatening to rain however, so I was pleased for the lift.

At stark contrast to the surrounds of the waiting room, hulking chunk of man sat quietly in one of the seats, covered in tattoos from head to toe. The veterinary nurse was casting terrified looks to anyone who made eye contact. Her hands shook as she mopped the floor around the room, notably avoiding a three-metre radius around the man.

Clearly Damien had already organised the man who would take the body, which would be much to Dr Celeste's relief. The poor man stood out painfully in such a high-class suburb and given the looks the nurse and the receptionist gave me, I wasn't seen in much of a better light. I ignored them and stood by the door while Damien quickly gave some instructions to the body courier.

As he walked to the door, Damien gave me a dimpled smile that I couldn't help but return.

'What will happen to the body now?' I asked, curiousity dominating my better sense.

'Seein' as we ain't sure who it is, gonna give 'im the ritual of death, then we gotta bury 'im. But Imma keep track of it if 'fen we find them's family,' Damien explained as he held the door open for me. I was impressed, and too loose to conceal my look of surprise.

'You take care of them that good?' I chirped in surprise as I trotted across to his car.

'Not all of 'em,' Damien said with a conspiratorial look. 'But the innocent ones, they done nothin' wrong. This one ain't deserved what he got. But gonna make sure his spirit gonna rest easy.'

I was speechless. This was a long way from the man I had first met, his attitude changing in a matter of days. I quickly climbed into the car to cover my shock and lack of response.

Chapter Twelve

The drive to the K-Hole was quick and painless. A comfortable silence had settled around us. Part of me itched to break it, but it made a nice change. We arrived without issue, even finding parking nice and close to the club. An industrial track pounded out of the door and into the night, making me grin with anticipation.

This was not just about work; I genuinely had a good time here. As I went to join the queue and pay my entry fee, Damien scooped me up. Placing a casual arm around me, he guided us directly to the door. The bouncer sneered over at us, but as soon as he spotted Damien, his face became a mask of professionalism.

'Aye Dame, ye got a woman fer tonight yeah? Gonna test out the facilities before ye buy eh?' His face was contorted into a smile, and I was disappointed in Damien that he was just using me for a sexual thrill at the K-Hole. I tried not to let it show under my own professional mask.

'Aye, the Lady in tonight?' Damien spoke with a glib air, revealing nothing of his thoughts. The bouncer simply nodded, so rather than stick around for more riveting conversation, I allowed Damien to lead me into the club.

Lights pulsed and writhed as the semi clad bodies on the full dance floor did the same. The heavy music hammered away at my soul, swamping my senses with a sexual tattoo. Damien caught my attention with a gentle touch.

'I thought ye might be better not payin' fer the door fee tonight eh? Save yer money.' I couldn't help the surprised glance at him. 'What, ye be thinkin' Imma take advantage of the fact ye be workin' tonight?

Naw, I ain't be doin' that. Ye got yer own work. I got mine ter do. Gotta go see'n 'em dragon lady. Ye be safe.' Damien nodded and walked away before I could formulate a response. I was genuinely speechless again, a moment that rarely happened except for around Damien. Apparently, this man brought it out of me.

Slowly the pulse of the music worked its way back into my dulled senses. There was something I was here to do. I wasn't scrubbed up so well to simply attend impromptu autopsies with belligerent gang lords. Time to go to the day job.

Procuring a client at the K-Hole might be safer, but unfortunately I was limited in how I could use my faery skills. Hypnosis and suggestion was forbidden, and marshals kept a close eye on things. The best bets were trying to get a client into one of the private rooms, or actually cough up the goods, figuratively speaking. Still, I had to get a nibble before I could set the hook and figure out the best way to reel a little fishie in.

Descending the stairs to the dance floor, the aura of sensuality became tangible. There was at least one lust spell in use, as well as traditional scents of seduction. There had to be other fae here, but I couldn't place where they were. This was the part of the job that I actually enjoyed. The music seeped into my skin, and I began to dance. Taking my chance to just enjoy the moment, I closed my eyes and just moved. The casual touches of other dancers sent fire sparks across my flesh. Together we all pulsed, pounded and pressed, body to body. This was the closest I got to freedom.

It was barely a minute into the second song before a stench shattered my peace. Before me stood a corpulent creature, with many visible chancres and a pervasive odour. I struggled to keep a professional mask up while trying not to gag. He flashed me a single fifty dollar note before grabbing my wrist with a sweat slicked hand. He began to pull me towards the slightly more private booths around the edges of the dance floor. Should it have been a more desirable male I would have been happy to oblige. Heck, none of it would matter if I could do my little trick. But not this man, not for a single fifty.

As it was, there was no way I was touching any part of this man. Using his sweaty nature against him, I slid my hand free from his grasp. Looking back at me, he began to swear loudly, insisting I follow through with his mediocre transaction. Before he could angrily march one step in my direction, the security swooped on him and swiftly removed him from the venue after confirming with a nod from me. This was why I liked this venue so much. It may be one sleazy step above a cheap brothel, but there was an excellent emphasis on safety for me. Still, how had he even been allowed in was another matter. Sweat aside, he clearly had syphilis.

Slightly rattled by the rather physical encounter, I popped another opiate pill in my mouth and let it soothe me back into the beat of the music. When I felt comfortable in my own skin again I opened my eyes and began to search for prey in this sea of fishies. Merely a few steps away, a rather young man was dorkily dancing away, all gangly arms and legs. He looked barely of age, but thankfully that was another nuance the venue took care of.

Everyone had to be of age, no exceptions. He glanced up at the upper walkways, and I followed his gaze. A clearly wealthy man stood watching on, older, enough to be the father. Ahh yes, the age-old solution for an awkward virgin son and a daddy with a pocket full of cash. Here was my perfect prey for the night.

I circled in like a shark, completely focused on my little minnow, angling to get in before anyone else noticed him. My movements were now fluid, softened by the beat and pills. As the poor lad noticed me approaching he blushed a deep red. It was kind of adorable. He was even a bit of a looker, the eyes of a dreamer, long but clean hair. A far better prospect than the previous man. We danced together for a song or two while he plucked up the courage to talk to me. Finally, he leant in to whisper to me.

'You are so pretty! My da- I came here to meet someone who could-um how much?' He stammered and stuttered, but I didn't laugh. He deserved that dignity at least.

'Depends on what you want and how long you want it for, but I have the whole night I can dedicate to your... mission.' I responded saucily and bit my lip. His blush darkened as a gorgeous grin broke across his face.

'Well, I don't know how long it will be, but I got a private room here. The, um, Fantasy Suite. Dad said- I was told that might sweeten the deal.' The young man sounded much more confident this time. I made sure to gently brush against his body as we were dancing. His little jerks of surprise was thrilling, as was the sizeable erection he was now sporting.

'You heard right my dear. That Fantasy Suite has everything you need for the best night in. Say $600 and I will make sure you have the best first... impression, of the room.'

'D-deal. Let's go!' He exclaimed with a small sigh as my hands wandered, and body pressed against him. Grabbing his hand, I lead him through the sea of flailing limbs and sweaty lust. Before disappearing into the corridor to the private rooms, he took one look back to the father figure for a reassuring nod.

We went straight down the hall to the hallowed end door. The Fantasy Suite was a wonder. A clean bed with satin sheets, chilled drinks readily available and plenty of slap and tickle accoutrements ready to go. As far as workplaces went, this was my favourite, especially with nervous rich men.

I stalked over to him, running my hands closer and closer to his belt. He bent in to kiss me, which surprised me so much I took a step back. A look of mortification crossed his face, so I stepped in closer again, moving my hand up to the back of his head.

'Are you sure you want to do this? We could just pretend...' I let that thought slide as he shook his head.

'I, well I didn't when I came here. I was so afraid. But you are so pretty and nice to me. I want to now, if that is OK?' he asked shyly. I smiled as he blushed up to his shock of thick hair yet again. Hair to run fingers through, with just a gentle tug as he... Decision made, I kissed him long and hard before pulling him towards the bed.

As much as I considered enchanting the man the second we had walked into the private room, I was glad I hadn't. The lad had proved to be a wonderful surprise, well-endowed and eager to learn to please and be pleasured. I sent him away with a few tips on how to satisfy a future girlfriend. He even seemed to have a happy father now. It was a bizarre rite of passage, but certainly not uncommon. I skipped out of the club as the K-Hole was closing, heavy in coin and a long trek back to Stevie's rooms. Luckily I had new shoes, and the sun was coming up. My walk ended without incident, and after a quick shower I gratefully collapsed into bed.

Chapter Thirteen

Dreams came and went, sometimes trailing into nightmares of emaciated bodies. Thankfully I still awoke well rested and unfortunately, to a dead phone. Having rarely owned one, I had forgotten to automatically charge it. I groaned as I plugged it in and fetched my stash tin. A quick morning pick me up and I felt almost... fae.

I inspected myself in the bathroom mirror to make sure there was no traces of last night's exertions, but the clever boy had left no trace. The thought of doing eye liner briefly crossed my mind but I couldn't be bothered. Hopefully today would bring some makeshift autopsy results. It wasn't worth the make-up. I also had to get to the library, and there was no one to impress there.

As my phone started up in the other room, notifications started pouring in. Checking its clock revealed that I had slept until 5pm, which was easy to do when you finally had a bed. Long sleep ins were non-existent on the streets. The first message that popped up was from Stevie.

'Some deaf woman bin here for ye. Ye want her number?'

He followed up with:

'Dumb woman don't wanna give it out. Somethin bout no calls. Told her to come back tonite then.'

A groan escaped my lips when I realised that Sadie probably didn't want to take calls because she couldn't hear them. Stevie could be pretty dense himself at times. I messaged back an OK before looking at the rest. Jojo had apparently sent a similar message, adding that Sadie would be back around 6pm.

Reminded by Sadie's connection to Martina, I dug her card out of the pocket of my jeans. It had gotten sweaty and creased up, but her number was still legible. *What a blessing*, I gleefully thought as I entered it into my phone. Despite my eagerness, I didn't feel confident enough to send a message yet. Instead, I read those beautiful numbers over, admiring how pretty a combination it was.

That thought ran a shiver of worry through me. In all my years of being on the streets I had avoided any kind of entanglement. Not even a crush had crossed my mind. Emotions made things too complicated. *Had these soft surroundings turned me soft too?* That made me vulnerable. Huffing and puffing about it wasn't going to get me anywhere though.

As I was dressing, I realised that the library was likely closed thanks to my sleep in. Annoyed at myself, I kicked aside a small decorative basket. It hit the wall with a sad little thud and fell to the floor. Now I felt guilty about destroying part of the immaculate room, which raised my ire some more.

What did a drug lord and gang leader want with a silly little basket? Why was Stevie doing any kind of interior decorating? This wasn't a hotel.

My thoughts compounded aggressively, a swirling mess now rampaging unfettered. Stopping myself short of screaming aloud, I threw some more pills in my mouth and checked my stocks. I wasn't out yet, but I had been burning through them fast lately. Stevie would likely want an update anyway, and I had last night's payment burning a hole in my pocket. I grabbed my key and money. No sense in taking an almost flat phone down the hall, so I left it there to charge some more.

Luck must have been with me tonight, because Stevie was in his office for once. I hadn't expected him to be in for the night yet.

'Aye Jessie. What been doin' eh?' he asked as I walked in, signalling for the door to be closed.

'Well, I have a few theories about all of this. For one, I think the spell aspect of the drug only works on men. Seems like they cop it, but I think women aren't affected.' I was interrupted in the middle of my rehearsed monologue by Stevie putting his hand up.

'Aye, that ain't be true now.' He grumbled. I stopped dead, feeling like my best theory had just been blown out of the water. Fear made my stomach writhe like a beheaded snake. Stevie nodded at my shock. 'Nathaniel done contacted me. Had a woman go and walk out of one of his rooms. Asked me to get you to go there when you are up.'

'I will go there as soon as I meet with Sadie. She should be here soon. Well, I guess the rest of my theories don't matter right now then.' I couldn't help but let the dejection I felt slip into my voice.

'Naw, don't be like that. Lemme hear what else ye got, eh?' I had to hand it to Stevie, the man had respect. It made the self-loathing dissipate just a little.

'Well, one of the victims has a twin. I am sure that I can use some kinda faery magick to use that link. I remember reading about something once to do with family links. I need to go to the library to check some books, but it's closed already.' I finished as Stevie chuckled.

'Library? Books? Y'all can use the internet fer that. Ain't no closin' times there.' He clearly seemed tickled at my presumed faux pas.

'Oh no, this particular author loathes technology. She eschews any part of the internet; says she can't trust it.' I replied, slightly hurt at the implication that I was a luddite in some way.

'Ye but surely someone gotta put somethin' up now. They got everythin' there.' Stevie seemed now interested, if his voice was anything to go by. Who would have thought Stevie was a tech-head?

'Nope, she has a curse woven into her words! If anyone tries to share any part of the book, they instantly cannot remember the details. It cannot be scanned, nor can pictures be taken. The older faeries are a lot like that! Some will not even allow humans to read their books!' I knew the kind of magick required to do such things and couldn't help but get breathless in my awe.

'Aye sounds stupid to me. Damned ridiculous idea.' He was now sulking in the face of the monolith that was faery paranoia.

'Er yeah. So, what you got stashed away? Got a little cash ready to spend.' As usual I was playing for a better deal. Stevie nodded before delving into a drawer beside him.

'How much you got girl?' he asked gruffly, suddenly all business.

'Only got $300, been busy with this case,' I replied, trying my best to sound tired.

'Aye, gimme the cash and I set ye up good.' He responded, weighing out bags on a tiny scale. I pulled out my pre-prepared roll of cash and handed it over. He nodded and tossed over a bountiful pack of pills. 'So why this deaf chick rock up? Had a real looker with her too. But ye ain't be bringing random wimmin in. Ain't no wimmin's refuge,' he mumbled, blushing about what he had said.

'Not at all, it's about the case Stevie. She is a friend of one of the victims, and one of the few women I know for sure has taken Faerie Fizzer and been unaffected. The other one, I guess it must have been Liselle. She translates for Sadie.'

'Aye Liselle eh? Yeah, ok, will tell the boys to let 'em in when they be comin' back. Ain't be long now, almost six.' Stevie mentioned as I glanced at the clock.

I jumped out of my chair fast when I saw it was ten to six, dropping my precious baggie as I went. I scooped it up, took my leave and bolted back to my room without saying goodbye. I had wanted to organise my pills before Sadie got here, to collect my thoughts. Now I had to go deal with the crushing of my favourite and only theory about female victims of the drug.

My first impression of Nathaniel had been awful, so I wasn't looking forward to the next meeting. Luckily I managed to throw my things together in time and was tying up my hair when someone knocked at my door.

I threw it open, expecting to see Jojo, but instead I encountered the most muscular, Amazonian woman I had ever seen in my life.

'You're a-.' I stopped suddenly as she gave a terrifying scowl.

'A what?' she growled.

'You're so fit! Like an Amazon! So powerful.' I responded, glad for the lucidity to correct my faux pas. She merely shrugged in response, but a creeping blush indicated that she had liked that comment. 'Where is Jojo?' I threw in.

'Off tonight. Got a lady love and he wants more time off. So, I got more work.' She said it as if I should know that she worked for Stevie already. I was pretty sure I had never seen her before, but I had come in worse for wear most of the times I came to Stevie's rooms.

'A lady love hey? Now that is interesting. Didn't think he was looking after the, you know...' I trailed off as I drew my finger across my throat, mimicking his injury. Gosh these pills made me dangerously chatty.

'Hah you think some girlfriend cut 'is throat? Naw that was our Mamma. Always said too many mouths to feed. I found 'im, patched 'im up and we done left that day.' The woman answered in such an odd matter that I temporarily forgot the important information there.

'Wait, Mamma? He is your brother?' I exclaimed, now understanding why this woman was so intimidating.

'Yep, mah lil brother, all grown up. Raised on the streets. I was always the big one, protected us, then one day he all grew up. Ain't no one wanna mess with us then. Got us a tidy thing goin' on.' I nodded, then she suddenly stopped and stiffened. 'Aye so the... uhhh... Sadie is here lookin' fer you.' Too much chatter.

'Oh, of course.' I grabbed my bag and ran out, slamming the locked door. Then I realised I hadn't gotten Jojo's sister's name. 'Sorry, if you have mentioned it before, what is your name?'

'Aye, Deanna,' she answered before lumbering off up the hall. The woman was a weapon.

Sadie and Liselle were sitting in one of the smaller waiting rooms, luckily free of anyone waiting to use the smoking rooms. Stevie was apparently attempting to serve them drinks, withering under a shrewd gaze from Liselle. He attempted to seem unperturbed by the glare, excessively simpering and smiling. Sadie looked up quickly when I entered. She hit Liselle in the arm and began signing rapidly.

'Why did ye not tell me dere is dead bodies bein' found? Is it him?' Translated Liselle as she hushed Stevie with a hand up.

'Bodies?' I exclaimed, shocked. 'I was aware of only one. That man was white, it wasn't Martine.' Sadie looked relieved before signing some more.

'Yeah, some street kids found hidden bodies today, said more were found that done looked the same. Dey don't want to tell anyone. Can't get them to talk. Need you to talk to 'em.' Liselle looked surprised and signed something to Sadie. Sadie nodded in response. 'Sadie didn't tell me 'bout no dead people. She just grabbed me and dragged me here. Ain't nothin' 'bout no dead folks.' Liselle admitted, a real sadness in her pretty eyes.

'Well, I will see what I can do I guess. So, they found a stash of bodies. Oh no.' Tears threatened to surge, but the numbness held them at bay. The shock held my mind paralysed. I know the silence was stretching off to an unprofessional level, but the moment of helplessness felt overwhelming. Sadie signed something, a gentle look on her face.

'I can see this be a surprise fer ye. Ye need to meet me tomorrow ter talk ter this kid. Wait, Sadie, ye know I have ter study tomorrow. Got an exam. I can't be helpin' ye.' Liselle interrupted the translation. Sadie snapped her fingers impatiently. 'Oh, Sadie says ye can still meet her, don't need to talk much. Ye can send her a message on her phone yeah? Can tell ye where ter meet then. This be her number,' translated

Liselle, passing me a dirty slip of paper with a number on it. Her hand trembled violently. 'Anything else new?'

'Well, I thought it was only men being affected by the drug, but now a woman has gone missing. Sadie, are you absolutely sure that you and Martine took the same drug?' I tried to ask as innocuously as possible.

'Aye, they split it 'tween them. Both taken th' same. Whatsit mean?' Liselle asked. I wasn't sure if it was her or Sadie asking this time. Feeling stuck, I rubbed my eyes with my palms.

'I don't know. Will go ask Nathaniel what information he has for me. Tonight. Now.' I replied with a groan as I checked my phone and realised that this was going to seriously cut into my other work time. Sadie saw my look and nodded. Liselle translated her parting words.

'It's terr'ble, people are scared. We pretend it's all ok. But ain't no one feelin' like dey got control now. Ain't no one got an idea who gonna be next.' With that, Sadie stood and walked out, her head held high, but tears were clearly running down her face. Liselle muttered something I couldn't catch, nodded at Stevie and followed her friend.

I sat there numbly, still holding the ragged piece of paper. Stevie began rambling some inane blather about Liselle, but I tuned him out. Sadie was right. No one had any idea who was next, or how to stop this. It was all out of control.

Chapter Fourteen

When I had gathered my thoughts, going to Nathaniel's place had taken top priority. I had to know more about why a woman would suddenly be affected when none other had. The walk over was taken up by updating and rereading my notes carefully to not miss any detail. There was something in all of this. I just had to plot it out.

Nathaniel's doorman was suitably dour; however, they brightened up the second I mentioned the reason for me being there. He showed me in with a bow and led me to Nathaniel. We ended up in the same room, gaudy in a fashionable way. This time Nathaniel was draped over a different man, who looked suspiciously like a myopic accountant. I couldn't help but be surprised when he was introduced as Nathaniel's husband. I stammered slightly, not wanting to point out that Nathaniel had been curled up to another man last time. Canny as he was, Nathaniel spotted my awkwardness.

'Yes, he too was my husband. We are a throuple. No cheating here! You would be terrible at poker sweetheart.' With that they burst into peals of laughter, clearly warming up to me. Or perhaps they wanted something.

'Oh, um, congratulations. I didn't realise you were married!' I chose my words carefully, not wanting to insult this man. The information he held was too precious.

'Yesh, married with children. Johnny raises them. Jackson helps with the business. It works for all of us.'

I nodded carefully, wanting to get to the point. Nathaniel's strong lisp was hard to decipher. Luckily he continued. 'So, had us a woman go missing today, Lucille.'

'So, this Lucille, it was the same as the others? Took the drug, got up and left within hours?'

'Yes. Got her hands on it somewhere. Then was in our rooms and started to act odd. Suddenly jumped up and ran out, heading kinda south-ish.' As he spoke his shrewd eyes boring into me. Now I realised how clever this man actually was. He was carefully analysing my every move. Not to be trifled with, moreso than my kind dope Stevie.

'You understand how unusual this is yeah? Of the women who I know used it, Lucille was the only one affected. My theory about it affecting only men via attraction was wrong.' I pondered the repercussions quietly, when Johnny finally piped up.

'You know she is an absolute lesbian right? Complete stud. Could bench press more than most men.' He spoke in a polite and quiet voice, with just a trace of an exotic accent. I shook my head, starting to formulate my next theory.

'No... so she is attracted to women and physically strong. Perhaps that explains why it only worked on her.'

'Ye, she looks like a man most times too. Got 'em pants and button up shirts only. Found out the hard way, that one.' I managed to quell the laugh that bubbled up from that tidbit of a revelation. Perhaps I was getting better at this whole professionalism thing.

'We all did, baby.' Johnny was trying to be conciliatory, but the idea of a stud lesbian being hit on by this odd throuple made me snort slightly, which I desperately tried to turn into my next statement.

'She took off south-aways. This only happened a few hours ago? OK which room was it and can I get in there? Might be a magickal trail. Can track 'em y'know.' I babbled mindlessly in my awkwardness. Nathaniel had narrowed his eyes but seemed to let it pass.

'Hm indeed. I will show ye the room. Come on.' As he stood, I realised that he was both incredibly tall and wore massive platformed heels. I gawked a second too long. 'Yes, when you are the skinny gay kid, your sense of survival becomes a weapon. They took a lot from me but gave strength from spite. Come on.' He strode out of the room, trailed by flutters of some kind of expensive looking silky material. I said goodbye to the nigh-on-silent Johnny and followed.

'The lisp really adds to the gay cliche there. I bet they loved that.' I quipped, feeling more comfortable around Nathaniel, but instantly wondered if I was being too pert. His silent stare did not help as he stopped suddenly in the passageway.

'Well, I wasn't born like this. One day in school they beat me so badly it damaged my head. I woke up with a lisp. It never went away. Spent years avoiding S words. But why should I suffer for the result of the abuse? So, I just be me now.' I felt an admiration growing as he spoke and lead me to the rooms, stopping before a bright pink door. 'This is it. Rattle down some of those useless junkies. I need Lucille back. Smack some of their idiot heads together for all I care.' The admiration faded just as fast as it grew. The ruthless Nathaniel was back, but I had to retain my facade.

'She must be a very good friend to you all.' I spoke the words in what I hoped was a conciliatory manner.

'No, she is the one who birthed our beloved babies. Only wanted drugs in return. Need one more from the bitch and now she is gone. What a waste of time. Too much effort to find another desperate druggie dyke. Ugh. Find her.' With his parting slurs, Nathaniel flounced back down the hall. I was shocked. Genuinely, speechlessly shocked. He truly was without redeeming feature. While trying to gather my composure, I slowly pushed open the door.

Every single den, in every single town, always had rooms like these. Stark, bland, yet with comfortable looking places to lounge while making use of the services on offer. Only the colour changed. Nathaniel's seemed to be all chrome and white. Classy, but not practical with drugs involved. There were a multitude of stains in varying colours present. Some were clearly blood, but the others were best left to the imagination.

A few stragglers lay about the room, all looking dazed. I couldn't help but feel that at least I wasn't like THEM, even as I rustled through my bag for my own stash. The attendant coughed loudly, so I very obviously drew out my notebook instead. The talk with Nathaniel had me so off kilter that I forgot this was not a BYO event. Plus, I would be damned if Nathaniel was going to get a single cent of my money.

Starting to make a show of it, I wrote down some scribbles as notes, then marched over to question the attendant. The prickle of withdrawals at the edges of my consciousness would have to wait.

'Well then, what are you? The tax department?' He snapped cynically. I etched a fake smile into my face in the name of professionalism.

'Hi, I am Jessie, a private investigator looking into the missing persons in this area. I was hoping to ask a few questions.'

'Oh, that. I don't see the point but sure,' he muttered as he began to fidget with a pen. With curly hair and the jawbone of a Greek statue, this man would be pretty attractive if he wasn't permanently frowning. His displeasure was clearly absolute. He had to have botoxed away the grouchy forehead wrinkles.

'The woman who just left, Lucille, what did she do just before she left?' I asked distractedly as I began to sense the trail of magick running through the room. He snorted, contorting his features into an even uglier visage.

'You call THAT a woman?' He snickered to himself, clearly feeling like that was a clever quip.

'Yes actually, what exactly would you call her? Actually, I don't even want to waste the brain cells sacrificed trying to talk to you.' As soon as I had locked down the magickal trail I snapped at him and walked out. There was no sense in trying to find out more information, he had likely thought Lucille beneath his attention. I was utterly revolted by every interaction in the place today, so a sense of relief ran through me when the trail went directly out of the rooms.

Bursting out to another cloudy evening felt like such a relief. The magick pulled me south-east if my inner compass was correct. I followed, drawing it into myself as I marched onwards. Turning it over and over inside of me, I analysed its etheric scent, taking in its unique signature. Every part became imprinted on my memory. The source was definitely fae, however it felt like there was more than one faery involved in crafting this spell. At least two threads were snarled together.

I wove through the scrappy crowds in this area, carefully dodging any intruding magicks crossing my path.

Soon the streets were almost deserted as I crossed into the industrial region. Even though I was coming in from another angle, I realised I was close to the area I had entered last time, before I was attacked. This memory made me slow my pace, looking carefully down each alley and nook.

The trail grew more intense, becoming almost discordant. A cacophony of internal noise began to build, and I was instantly reminded of the music lessons where we had learnt about the Devil's tri-tone. I automatically brought my hands up to cover my ears. It was all in vain as the wretched sound bore into the recesses of my mind, being magick and not sound. This distraction allowed a man to slip up behind me before I even noticed.

'Hello, my pretty little peach. What might you be doing out here? You are all alone, and dusk is falling fast and... hard.' He said with a leer.

This was not your standard Bayton slum stock. The man before me had a slightly rumpled and scuffed suit on, including a tie. His teeth were in perfect condition and accent was free of the verbiage of the slums. This man did not belong in South Bayton.

'I was just cutting through, need to get to the other side. Ain't got nothing to steal, just working the streets, but ain't done it yet.' I tried to seem as innocent as possible, just a broke sex worker looking to get paid.

'Nah my little minx, no one just cuts through here. You should know that.' He spoke slowly as he walked ominously closer to tower over me. The effect was certainly intimidating enough, and I stumbled a step or two back.

'I usually work the K-Hole, but my friend told me there's a bunch of rich folks in that far South border of Bayton and Gaynesboro lookin' to spend money on new faces.' I desperately lied as the prickling from the withdrawals intensified. The big guy continued to slowly step closer, and I realised that he was backing me up into an alley. I had to move fast.

'Naw girly, you can't be here. This is not the area for pretty little butterflies to flutter into. They are so delicate, and this is the kind of place that they get crushed in rough hands.' He growled now, voice low and vicious. I switched method.

'Well perhaps you are looking for some good company as the dusk falls? You are such a big, handsome man. Look at these strong arms.' I purred as I stepped forward and attempted to run my hand up his arm. He pulled back quickly, refusing to make skin contact. *Interesting. This man was not fae but was certainly acting as though he knew our ways.*

'Don't even try it little butterfly, I will tear those wings off.' He shoved me to the floor. The contact was too brief to ensnare him, and I went down hard. Elbows hit concrete and its grains dug in hard. I felt the skin break and prayed I would not leave blood lying around. It was too easy to curse someone with. I couldn't tell what else was injured yet, but my head spun with the pain.

I scrambled back to my feet as he advanced on me again. He was unbuttoning his shirt, for what I had no idea. Even if he intended to get his rocks off, that much contact would allow me to entrance him.

His eyes flashed with not anger, but magick. I could see an iridescent pink sparkle deep in his pupils, the colour of the magick pulling his strings. Fae magick. I lurched towards him, feeling too bruised to try to stand and fight. He seemed to be taken by surprise, and I managed to grab hold of him. My mind was too unfocused to snare him, and that damned noise broke my concentration. This time we both went down.

Luck must have been with me this time as I managed to retain my position atop the attacker. Mustering all that was fae and powerful within me, I slammed my bare palm down onto his solar plexus and released a flood of magick. I had his mind within nanoseconds and shut him down.

My head began to throb as a wetness dripped down my back. My breath burned through my lungs, both from exertion and the heat that pure fae magick generated. Carefully, I raised my hand to my head, feeling through my dreadlocks. Sure enough, I found blood and lances of pain from some kind of wound. A haze began to frost over my eyes as I lurched off the unknown man, desperately reaching for my bag. Its contents spilled as I scrabbled for my phone. Luck was with me as it fell into my hand easily for once. I shakily dialled Damien's number and mentally begged the call to connect before the darkness claimed me. It rang and rang as my eyes closed, but a faraway voice still said hello. I used the last of my consciousness to plead for help.

Chapter Fifteen

Awareness came slowly but painfully. The lights burned into my closed eyelids from above me. I must be laying down. Opening my eyes proved hard, and many weak attempts resulted in failure. Finally, the noises of the room around me started to sink in. There were voices, warm and soft. Words hovered just beyond comprehension. I strained my ears to listen but all I could determine was that Damien was probably one of the speakers. Eventually I simply resorted to groaning.

'Aye that be goo-... Doctor done said you-... be restin' up an'-... ok lass?' The first voice she heard clearly likely belonged to Damien. Try as I might, I could not hear all the words. I groaned again in response. Suddenly I felt too tired to care. The details would have to wait. Sweet sleep carried me off again.

The second time I awoke was significantly harder. Tremors exploded through my body, caused by fully withdrawing from the usual blend of drugs in my system. I wanted to vomit, but my mouth was completely dry, resulting in a whole lot of rasping pain. Struggling to sit before I even opened my eyes, I came to a teetering state of horizontal-ness. My eyesight was blurred, but I could tell there was multiple people in the room.

'B-bag. Need my bag,' I stammered, trying to get my mouth to work. Someone handed it to me. I desperately dug through the contents to find my pills. My purse felt intact, and that was quite a relief. There was still a good chunk of money in there from my work at the K-Hole.

Passing out in the streets usually meant sacrificing all your valuables. My pills tin ended up falling out onto the floor as a result of my desperate hunting. Frustrated, I groaned loudly and swore. Before I could pick it up myself, Damien sat down next to me, handing over a glass of water as he picked up the tin.

There was conversation occurring around me, but I lacked the focus to really hear it. I crunched a few pills and put them under my tongue to dissolve as I swallowed others. My shakes slowly settled as my pain faded. As a result, my mind became clearer, to the point where I could finally make out words.

'See Steve, I bin lookin' after her. Ain't me that done nothin'. She just be callin' me, all bloodied up and I do what I can eh.' Damien spoke to a dark blur over in the corner of the room.

Steve? Did he mean Stevie? What on Earth, Stevie would never go to Damien's turf, it was just not done. When the blur answered, it was unmistakable.

'Ah Damien, ye know I just got caught up worryin'. Hasn't been safe lately. Ain't want Jessie caught up in it. She ain't part o' this fight.' Stevie intoned in a low pitch, keeping his words short and clear. Damien shrugged as he leant back onto the couch awkwardly in his armoured jacket. The blur of it looked like a bright red, with some deep gold pattern.

'Naw, I know she ain't in this. Just keepin' her safe in my lands. The rest be between ye an' me. We got that clear.' The Damien blur turned to me. 'How ye doin' Jess? Head be feelin' better?' he asked me carefully.

'Yeah... that hurt. I hit my head. Had a fight with some guy. He was controlled by the one making the drugs. There is definitely something in that area.' I responded gingerly. My head still throbbed, but it was much better. 'How did you know where I was though?'

'Well, I heard ye need help, and ye have a mobile phone. Got them find yer phone things and had me men there fast. Even got both of ye picked up.' Damien took the empty glass from me and went to refill it. My vision was finally starting to clear.

'What are you doing here Stevie?' I asked curiously.

'Ye didna come back fer two days Jessie, so I checked round. Someone said dey seen Damien's boys carryin' ye off and blood been on ye. So, I done called him up lookin' fer answers. He ain't be answerin' so I come here meself.' Stevie had an oddly caring grin on his face, but not in a creepy or romantic way. The fact that he thought to check up on me was rationalised in my mind as that he didn't want to lose his link in this little investigation. There was no way anyone actually *cared* about me. That was it.

'Thanks Stevie. A guy got the jump on me while I was chasing up the woman who got taken. It... uhhh, turns out that it was probably for the same reason,' I finished awkwardly. I couldn't help but feel a lack of confidence about my theory.

'What ye meanin' same reason?' Damien asked as he passed the glass back to me. I gratefully accepted it.

'Well apparently she was a very masculine lesbian. I think the faery who is doing this has cast the spell to attract anyone strong who would be attracted to them. So being that kind of target person, well it worked on them. That's what I think, anyway.' The men simply nodded, without making any quips or comments.

That impressed me. I had expected rude jokes or something derogatory, especially from Damien, however I was pleasantly surprised. Feeling that two of the most powerful men in Bayton were actually listening to me was odd. 'They know I am looking for them now. I am sure of it after today- erm two days ago. That man knew to avoid being touched, and how long he had to touch me when he did. Where is he now?' I dropped the question in casually, trying to make it seem like a nonchalant question. The quick glance between Stevie and Damien put me on edge instantly.

'Yeah, dem. As soon as we got 'im in a room an' he woke up, erm, well... well 'e beat 'is head on de wall. Ain't stoppin' till 'e dead. Took only a few seconds, ain't nothin' could stop 'im. Damn made a mess.' Damien gave a pained grimace as he spoke. That made me feel as though there was some kind of heaviness in my stomach. I was currently too highly dosed to register specific emotions. Numbness was a blessing right now.

'So, nothing to trace. Of course. Guess they planned that too. Once again we have a general area, but no details.' I mumbled, feeling dejected with the progress. A few awkward seconds stretched out into painful minutes as I ruminated on the challenges facing us.

It was only then I remembered one last idea that had been floating around for a few days. I didn't want to interrupt as the men spoke between themselves. It was so weird to see the two talking in such a civil manner. I reached over to my jacket that was draped across a simple wooden side table and pulled it slowly over. The movement alone flared enough pain to make me wince dramatically. Next was my bag, dragged up from the floor and onto my shoulder.

I lurched to my feet, my legs wobbling aggressively.

'Tha fuck yer think yer doin' Jessie? Ye got head wound n' all,' snapped Stevie.

'Have to get to the library. Need to research twin links. Only I can do it.' The words came out in short sentences while I tried to get the coordination together to walk.

'Can't ye just be lookin' it up online?' Damien asked dubiously. Clearly he expected me to just collapse on the spot. I wasn't that weak yet. Especially not when Martine was still out there and I had to help Martina.

'No, it's in a specific faery book. It is not online at all. We keep this stuff very secret but protected in public places like libraries. Faery magick is something unique to us, and we want to share it with other fae, but not broadcast our secrets to everyone.' I lectured as the swaying slowed down and numbness descended on my body once again. Stevie looked convinced having already had this talk, but Damien still had a tense expression on his face. I brushed it off as I headed to the door. 'Goodbye guys, will catch you at ho- in the rooms Stevie.'

Both men grunted a response and thankfully ignored my faux pas of calling the borrowed room a home. I felt like I should thank Damien a lot more given that he had come to my rescue, but it just felt weird to do so in front of Stevie. Holding my chin as high as I felt able to, I limped from the room and down the hall. The main armoured door was blessedly opened for me by some meaty muscle for hire. The glare from the little shopping complex burned into my eyes, a blinding light that seared my retinas. I blinked away the tears that welled in response furiously, lest someone think I was crying.

The limp over to the library was suitably drawn out and painful. Multiple times I was jostled around by crowds of people too preoccupied with their own situations. By the time I reached the Bayton Central Library I was aching fiercely. The automatic glass doors were covered with myriad greasy hand prints of all sizes. The librarian was a surprisingly burly man, hunched over his small desk. Gentle fingers tapped away at his tablet computer as he scanned books in and placed them into a foam lined cart. Someone at a book shelf to my left dropped a book, which loudly clattered to the floor. The librarian's head whipped around to face the culprit. There was a gasp and the poor girl dropped to the floor to pick the book up. She smoothed out the cover gingerly and showed him there was no damage done. The librarian simply grunted in response and returned to his work. The whole interaction was done in a matter of seconds but impressed on me greatly the type of man he was.

As the young girl scooted across to the copious amount of chairs available, I stepped up to the main desk.

'Um hello. I am needing the faerie section.' I felt nervous as I asked. He slowly looked up at me with hazel eyes glaring out under a shiny bald head.

'The faery section huh? What makes you think that fantasy shite is real? Ye be looking fer werewolf, witchie and vampire books next. Ain't no little fluttering faerie books here.' He asked with a guttural snigger. Shock held my tongue. Everyone in the faerie community said that the local libraries held a faerie section, along with the other non-mundane groups. This was a way they could share encoded information to be accessed as needed in a public archive. I had never had a need to actually check before though. Bile rose in my throat as unease made me take a step back. *How would I find out a way to help Martina now?*

The librarian shook slightly and looked up at me, lifting his chin this time. This allowed me to see the silver sheen in his eyes, surrounded by laugh lines. The cheeky bastard was fae! I stood there with my jaw agape, words lost completely as he roared with laughter. Based on his size alone I would never have guessed he was one of us, but clearly he had to be. There was no way to fake that change in eye morphology that was unique to the fae. By this time, he had tears running down his face as he stood up and handed over a key card.

'This will allow you access, go to the lifts in the lobby and tap this card on the reader before selecting floor three. It is the only way you can get up there. Hand it back to me at the end though. If you take it outside or keep it for more than 12 hours, the card will deactivate. There will be another librarian on the floor if you need any help.' He couldn't keep the smirk off his face about his little trick, and I was forced to begrudgingly laugh along.

The security was entirely necessary as it turned out. What I had thought would simply be a small section of encoded books in the main library ended up being an entire floor dedicated to fae culture and history. The glorious books with their magickal encoding held secrets of the fae craft, that humans were banned from knowing. Many elements of their ways had to be kept secret, especially when it related to their effect on humans. They tended not to like books that talked about exploiting unwary humans.

All of the books were wonderful, tome after tome of pride for faery culture, tales of prominent fae in history and incredible magickal milestones. The urge to spend time reading all of these beautiful facets of myself was overwhelming, but I knew I had to keep going. I was going to need a book about powerful fae magick, to hypnotise a person and hijack their mind in order to walk the link to their twin. I was also going to need it fast, as a quick check of my loudly beeping phone revealed a message from Martina that she could feel her brother weakening. The others perusing the books all glared over at me with silver flecked eyes. There was snorts and grumbles of annoyance until I realised that libraries generally disapproved of loud noises such as phones. Grinning awkwardly, I held up my hand apologetically as I put it on silent. Soon everyone returned to their browsing, but I could feel the flow of annoyed faerie magick and energy pulsing through the room.

Responding to the message that I was currently researching a solution, I started scanning the genres with greater haste. Finally, I found an entire aisle dedicated to faerie-craft, however there was now no indication which book I would actually need in sight. I was floundering.

As if drawn by my flustered energy, a petite fae man walked over. He wore the uniform of the Bayton Library, so I smiled in relief.

'I need a book.' I said a little too earnestly. He laughed. In my face.

'I figured that is what you are doing here.' His eyes sparkled with such a pleasant nature that I could not be annoyed by his glib response.

'No, I need a very specific book about twin links and hypnosis with fae magick. Specifically used together.'

'Oh, I see. That is very specific. Have you looked online if that exists?' He asked carefully and politely. Confusion clouded my way. I knew what online meant but hadn't really thought about such things. I shook my head. 'Ok, you have a phone, yes? Hand it over.' Despite having a soft, careful voice, a hint of the Bayton accent still flowed through his words.

I silently drew the phone out of my bag while he directed me to a comfortable seating area. The way he gracefully folded his body into the couch made me feel incredibly uncomfortable. This man certainly embodied what it meant to be fae more than I could ever hope for.

The memory of my maternal grandmother's disgust at my lack of grace and decorum burned its way through my barriers. I had never been good or beautiful enough to be fae enough. I was lucky to have inherited the fae magick strongly, as everything else came from my much-loathed father. Feeling suddenly intimidated by being in a room full of the fae, I awkwardly threw myself onto the other chair.

'Oh great, it's a new model! These are so expensive. Ooh I have wanted one of these for weeks. Anyway, you need to do a search for what yer want, but you gotta use the *other* network for it.' He chattered as he tapped away furiously on my phone. Again, confusion dominated my features.

'Other? There's multiple?' The question felt silly as it left my traitor mouth.

'Yes, there is even a specific region for the fae. I have added that connection to your phone now, so just tap here... this is the fun part! It live scans your pupils to verify that you are one of us! Isn't that amazing?' He gushed happily. I had to admit, it was impressive.

'So, it's totally safe? That really is fascinating.' I responded awkwardly. The librarian gave me an odd look but continued.

'So now we search what? Twin link... hypnosis, and fae magick? Ooh and you want a book. There we go. There is a few mentioned that might cover what yer need. Let me cross check that with what we have in stock.' He excitedly pulled out his own phone and started tapping. I realised at this point that I had no idea what his name was. I had certainly forgotten that social nicety in my rush. When he found what he was looking for, his delicate face lit up with a beautiful beam.

'Yes, here. We have "Tales of Faery Magick Throughout History" as well as "Faery Witchcraft and Science Today" which seem to cover parts of what you are looking for. Follow me.' He leapt out of his chair as he gave my phone back. Again, I was forced to lumber along behind him. This time I actively tried to keep my footsteps light like they had drilled into me in deportment classes. The streets had scoured much of this from me.

Soon I had those two books in hand, along with another three on general rituals and spell working. The wonderful fae librarian had bowed at my thanking him and disappeared off through the shelves, sensing another customer in distress.

Taking up a study table this time, I cracked the books and adjusted my sight to see the faery content. All of them were disguised cookbooks, and the text soon melted away to reveal the vibrant colours of faery texts. The magick was brought to life with rich details of magickal experiments, including the glamours and hypnosis. I soon realised that when I took the minds of clients and gave them their money's worth, I was already practising a rather high and powerful form of the hypnosis needed.

Now I needed to be able to keep the person conscious and guide them along while they were under, instead of just feeding them false memories and fantasies. There was also mention of twins, both historically and currently studied. This was more along the lines of telepathy, empath connections and even sympathetic healing, so it looked likely that this was a viable option. I took down all the notes I could including some helpful methods and herbs to facilitate the magick. This was going to be something ground breaking if I could make it work.

By the time I had enough notes to feel comfortable enough with what might work for the ritual, it was already heading into late afternoon. Returning the books was bittersweet, as was returning the access card to the delights of the fae library. I had so dearly wanted to stay and keep reading. Unfortunately work called me, as I was running short on cash and cigarettes. Messaging Martina had been a highlight to my afternoon however, even if it was just to find the perfect time to cast a great ritual and find her missing brother. Now it was time to work the late shift, as well as find these children that had supposedly found a stash of dead bodies.

I texted Sadie to explain about getting knocked out, and that I was still keen to talk to the children if they were still around. They didn't respond while I waited at the library for a drizzle of rain to stop, so I had to just lope off to work and hope she would be around.

Chapter Sixteen

I opted for the K-Hole again, rather than risk the streets. During the walk over I had looked for Sadie or even Liselle, but they were noticeably absent. Purchasing my way into the club, I settled in quickly, grabbing a drink and topping up my pills to get me through. Rather than hitting the dance floor so early in the night, I scored a table to review my notes.

My semi-lucid state allowed the information to float through my mind in a rather nebulous manner. The components of the ritual needed began to slot into place and I scribbled them down furiously. Soon I had a complete picture of what was needed, all intuitively gathered and combined with my research. The oddest sense of pride made me feel warm, prickly. The feeling was so unusual for me that I also felt tangibly uncomfortable at the same time. Instead of dwelling on the implications, I decided that it was clearly time for a new drink.

The bar was much fuller by now, with other sex workers plying their trade and shooting looks at each other over every man that stumbled in. The feeling of drama was rife, and a pair of highly glittered and feathered drag queens were already squabbling in a corner over a very embarrassed looking business man. I watched as he slowly backed away and slunk into the crowd, unnoticed by the queens. Some of the usual ladies that I recognised even seemed snappy. Overall, it was an odd feeling, so I avoided eye contact and instead made a line directly for my favourite bartender.

Ordering quickly, I had turned to survey the crowd for a potential match for tonight when a tall woman walked over awkwardly. She had hair of the softest brown that fell past her shoulders and glowing green eyes obscured by enormous glasses. Even without make up she was pretty, strikingly so, in such an unconventional manner. I was surprised when she stood before me.

'Can I buy that for you?' She spoke in a raspy voice so quiet that I could barely hear it over the music.

'Oh, um, sure! Thank you.' I was surprised at her offer of a drink, especially given the tension in the air tonight. She quickly paid and we stepped away to make room for others.

'I noticed you seem different to all the others here. Writing and things. So, I wanted to talk to you.' Poor thing was so awkward, it must have been one of her first nights in the trade.

'I haven't seen you here before, are you new here or just getting into... you know, the biz?' I asked before sipping on my drink. Her eyes widened innocently, looking more and more like a meadow dwelling doe. This woman deserved to be innocently sitting in a sunny meadow with a halo of flowers on her head, not sitting in a grimy sex club with wannabe gang bangers grinding away on sex workers because they couldn't afford a full service.

'Me? No. Uh I am here for other reasons. To... buy.' Her unusual voice broke off in a mutter. In fine form, I spit a little of my drink down my chin in shock.

'You are seeking a worker?' My voice was filled with a shock I could not conceal. Her face showed how utterly startled she was by my outburst, and I instantly felt remorse for my reaction. A blush was spreading across her face. I took my chance and grabbed her hand.

'Come with me.'

My evening dealt with and my income made; I took to the streets again to wend my way home. Pleasantly tipsy after such a lovely night made the walk a delight. The loveliness of my customer had left a thrill in my heart, and I had expressed my confusion at her need to purchase a night of love. She was bashful but felt comfortable enough to admit that she lived with family, a kind of family that would not accept her sexuality.

For years she remained celibate, until curiousity and need got the better of her. I was empathetic to her situation, having to cover up elements of my own sexuality with my paternal grandmother, for fear of being cut off. I slipped her my phone number at the end, not only for a repeat of the amazing night we had, but also for support. The thoughts of the night kept me company as I walked back to the Fox's Den just before dawn.

My happy rambling was broken by a small gang of men running up the street towards me. Initially I felt compelled to hide from them in an alcove, however a glimmer in the monolith made me stop. They were all showing that temporary pink eye glitter of the enchanted. I realised now that those enslaved by the faerie fizzer had taken on the eye sheen similar to that of the fae, but it was a sickly mockery of the real thing.

They showed no reaction to my presence, just stampeding by blindly. I moved to follow them but was instantly impeded by a second group of men, and then a third. There had been at least 14 men passing through within the space of a minute. I was shocked, realising that the situation had now advanced aggressively. My first instinct was to follow them and was forced to run as fast as my short legs could take me.

Despite knowing which direction they had gone, following the groups of men proved to be impossible. They wove through the streets as a unit. There was no need to communicate when their minds were controlled by a single entity.

Given that I had simply gone bolting off rather drunkenly, it was probably for the best. I had no plan and no back-up. What good would it be to storm my way in after them? Still, I tried to keep following them out of duty but had to concede defeat when the sun began to rise. There was no way I could keep up with drug-fuelled sprinting men in my condition.

Whoever was doing this had just scored a huge group of men. This was an incredibly bad sign. I swayed on my feet as I watched the sun rise some more. There was nothing I could do but limp back to my room and ferret away my earnings. There was a chill in the air in the early dawn, and Bayton had a sense of crispness. The freshness that the night had lent the city was burning off fast in the sun as its inhabitants began to surface.

The permanent pervasive stench was beginning to rise. My current surroundings of dull grey industrial zone gave way to bright graffiti and dark alleys. It was the kind of dramatic juxtaposition only the most destitute of urban areas can produce.

Relief warmed my frosty bones when I finally made it back to Stevie's rooms. As I latched the door to my room my legs finally gave out. I sank to the floor and was forced to crawl to my bed before passing out on top of the covers.

Chapter Seventeen

Just once, I wished I could wake up feeling well rested. There was no chance given the life I lead, but a fae can dream. The curse of grogginess clouded my senses from the moment consciousness found me. Having this pretty little bed and its soft crimson sheets didn't help as far as combating an insidious fatigue that went to the bone. Still, I managed to sit up, desperately forcing my pills into a dry mouth. They slowly drew away the fogginess, and I was able to find my phone.

For someone who had never owned one, I sure got addicted to this little glass and plastic monstrosity fast. Luckily there were no new messages for me, thus hopefully no new dead bodies, so I took the chance to message Martina. Now I had both a twin and a ritual, and if it worked, the possibilities were endless. We could do this. End it all.

Unfortunately, then my cushy room privileges would end too. As ostentatious as a crimson and gold themed room was, I had grown fond of it, especially the security. The fact that I now had spare money stashed away was odd enough. Fresh clothes, the ability to bathe, all of it was something I now did not want to lose.

Now I finally had something to lose. That felt like a kind of betrayal. Having small blessings only made the loss worse, and my sense of selfishness.

I had fallen so deeply into my introspection that the sound of my phone notification chime made me jump violently. A message from Martina popped up, followed by one from Stevie. I guiltily opened Martina's first.

Jessie, good to hear. Please come over ASAP. I can feel him fading. <3

The heart emoji made my own traitorous heart leap with promise. I tried to reason that she had probably meant it as a friendly gesture, some residual habit that leaked through to the person she thought could save her brother. Unfortunately, logic dared not intervene when it came to affairs of the heart. I quickly responded that I would be over as soon as my little legs would allow.

Stevie's message bore no direct news from this area; however, he mentioned that Nathaniel had lost a good chunk of men. Undoubtedly these were the crowds of men I had seen in the early hours of this morning. Twisting a ratty faerylock between my fingers as I replied helped to soothe the nerves running rampant through my mind. I had checked over my notes on what to do with this magick propelled hypnosis so many times that I had them memorised. Still, that did little to quash my nerves about both seeing Martina and being responsible for this little fishing experiment.

A shower and a pep up dose from my stash meant that I was out the door and feeling confident in less than half an hour. The walk over to Maydwell's Urban Grind was pleasant enough in the cooling afternoon. My carefully written notes were clung to my chest as I walked, now my most precious possession. Reciting the words of the spell to connect minds with Martina in the hidden faery language synced in time to my steps, a diversion to make the walk go faster. Still the sense of trepidation grew. I would give anything to make this work and see Martina happy again.

The door to the cafe felt unusually heavy, although I had to admit to the bias that my trepidation clearly added. The cafe itself had not changed. It was as warm and welcoming as ever, with a bustle of content patrons. When the front of house was staffed by a man I had not met before, I began to look around for Martina. When her familiar cloud of hair and cinnamon-warm skin was not immediately evident, I began to panic.

Suddenly the male barista seemed to notice I existed and summoned me with a frenetic wave of his hand. Fully expecting to be kicked out for vagrancy, I walked over quietly.

'Thank goodness you are here. Martina has been frantic. Please, she is in the kitchen. Go to her.' His smile was warm and genuine, freckles and upturned nose making the image even cuter. In contrast his voice and words were strained with urgency.

It was clear that even her employees cared deeply for her. I was equally amazed that none seemed to resent or be disgusted by my appearance. I had gotten so used to being kicked out of every quality establishment that I dared to enter that it was a shock to be treated like a human being. Perhaps the bathing helped, or just the good people.

'Thank you.' I kept my response simple, not wanting to waste the man's time when there was an extensive queue waiting eagerly. This adorable little cafe was definitely a successful one. I was forced to weave through the fully occupied tables and chairs in order to get to the swinging door of the kitchen.

Martina was sitting on boxes of soy milk, tiredness weighing down her entire demeanour. When I knocked tentatively and entered the room she looked up, hurriedly wiping out away tears and jumping to her feet.

'Jessie, thank you. I know you must be so busy, with so many men missing.' She held her voice steady, a testament to her strength. I simply admired her all the more. Janelle nodded from behind the stove, but continued cooking. They were clearly busy as hell.

'I am, but your brother may be the key to all of this. He is the only one with a link such as yourself. Well, that I know of. So that means you are pretty important to... me.' I couldn't help the visible cringe at my lame finish, but luckily Martina seemed too distracted to notice. Perhaps she simply had the grace to ignore it. Janelle, meanwhile, snorted quietly as she threw some hand ground herbs onto an enormous slab of meat. I glanced over at her, but she never returned the look. Small mercies.

Her smug grin on the other hand...

'Well, what do we need to do for this link? Martine feels so weak now, so defeated. I need to help him.'

'Apparently it is only some words by a faerie and a hypnotic state. But I need you to be absolutely comfortable and relaxed, it may take a while.' I explained, hoping that my voice carried the confidence I did not feel.

Bless her, she nodded sagely.

'Well, we better do it at home then. That will be the most relaxing place for me. We have privacy there too.' With that, Martina stood up, dusted off her already immaculate clothing and prepared to leave. Janelle hugged her tightly before pressing a small bag into my hand. It seemed to be filled with ground herbs. Luckily she caught my quizzical look without being insulted.

'If you need 'em, these are the most powerful herbs us folk have for getting things done. Magickally speaking of course.' This time I couldn't help having a few tears escape. I had no idea what the not-fae used in such circumstances, but I welcomed any help.

'Thank you. I will get this done.' I said, with absolute sincerity. Janelle nodded and turned back to her meat, hefting it into the smoky oven. I sniffled loudly and walked out of the kitchen, only to be handed a coffee and an enormous muffin. The barista of the day gruffly pointed out that it was for the energy needed to get Martine back to them. I managed to stifle a sob into a very undignified snort.

How do I tell these people that I was just some pathetic street faerie, playing at being professional so that she could live in her dealer's rooms? They were all so kind, and I was all so useless.

I carefully sipped the coffee, sweetened to perfection. I briefly wondered if he was psychic, knowing to heavily sugar my white coffee. He caught my appreciative smile and explained.

'I read that the fae like everything to be sweet. Figured you would like it that way, along with a pistachio and rosewater muffin.' He said lightly, turning back to the counter when someone rang the bell for service.

They knew what I was and researched for me.

People rarely thought of me. I was speechless. These people all went out of their way to know and help me. Tears made my eyes sting, but Martina was already halfway to the door. The sunlight streaming in from the window was framing her in a nacreous aura, or perhaps it truly was the pure goodness surrounding her. She was glorious, resonant and so bright it hurt my eyes. She was the sun, and I was the dull moon, weakly trying to reflect her glory.

I resorted to trotting to keep up, being a full head shorter than Martina meant that I had to almost take three steps to her one. Luckily it turned out that the twins lived only a street over, in a modernised industrial area. They owned an honest to goodness warehouse, one of the smaller ones that hadn't been converted into apartments. While the outside looked distinctly run down, complete with broken windows, the inside was clean, completely chic and very comfortable. They even owned Chesterfield couches with Persian rugs on the polished concrete floors.

My mouth was agape as I looked around at the gorgeous surroundings, unable to contain my awe. There was old medicine bottles and scientific laboratory equipment, multitudinous books arranged on stunning red wood book shelves and even some tasteful but quirky taxidermy pieces that Martina explained as being all ethically sourced. The whole space was utterly gorgeous.

After offering the customary refreshments, Martina got straight to the issue at hand.

'So, did we need to sit? Stand? What did you need?'

'Well sitting would be better, it may be a long process. I guess we could move this chair here...' Between the two of us, the lounge room was soon made into a workable space, and Martina was sat uncomfortably close to me. Our knees touched. 'Now, I want you to think of your brother. What he means to you. Emotions apparently are important for this kind of ritual, the magick responds stronger. So really feel how much you want to find him.' I explained, trying to sound professional yet again. Martina snorted.

'No fear of that, I certainly have the emotion there.' She settled into a comfortable pose and began to regulate her breathing at my request. I watched carefully, waiting for the sweet spot that I had read about, when that careful breathing became something unconscious, falling into a natural rhythm.

Martina was ready to connect to. The spell to do so was not particularly challenging, however its rhythmic nature enhanced the hypnotic state while facilitating the magickal connection.

While I had expected a slow transition into her mind, I actually snapped into it with speed that left me magickally reeling. I was equally shocked to realise that her mind had a *feel*. There was that warmth she naturally exuded, as well as a cloying sorrow pervading every space. Not wanting to invade her privacy, I made for the link to her twin as soon as I got my bearings. That part was easy. All I had to do was head for the radiating sense of pain and confusion. Travelling within a mind was an unusual feeling. It was a little like flying without any resistance. This journey took longer, probably because there was a significant physical distance to cover. The world eventually became clearer, emerging from the miasma of the unconsciousness. I became aware of toil, sweat and a pervasive feeling of exhaustion. The sun burned into my eyes, making my physical body flinch in pain. Heavily tattooed arms with dark skin extended before me, setting large bricks in place along a newly constructed wall.

Martina squealed suddenly, catapulting us back into our respective bodies. Tears were flooding down her face now, and she remained incoherent for a few minutes. Finally, she calmed enough to talk again.

'Those arms, that was his tattoos! Was that really him?'

'Yes, it should be him right this minute. We are seeing his surroundings exactly as he is right now, through his eyes.' I explained, hoping I was right. I felt frustrated at being shot back into my body just as I was making progress.

Still, Martina was ecstatic. I had to settle her down and start again. This time the transition was easier, and we were back in Martine's mind within seconds. This time we were flooded with a stench, sweat and excrement, death and bile. Martine seemed impervious to it, working on dutifully. His hands were cracked and bleeding, each rough brick stained with his blood. There was little to be gleaned from his surroundings that I could see from my limited perspective. There were other men, all working. Some delivered the bricks, others mixed cement. Martine never looked up, so I could get no further detail. He just worked.

Suddenly sobbing broke out, and I was again thrown into my own body. I looked at Martina, my annoyance at the interruption dissipating as I saw her pain.

'He was, he was so thin. The blood. His hands. He was never so thin. Why is he still working when he is bleeding everywhere?' Her words came jumbled into staccato sobs.

'Well, he must still be under the control of the spell. It keeps him a prisoner better than any walls. I couldn't see what he was building though. Did you notice anything that may help with locating him?' I asked hopefully. I couldn't let her see my frustration.

'No, I couldn't see anything. Just the blood. That is why he feels so weak. He just... oh no.' Martina broke into sobs again. This time there was no calming down, she simply had to cry it out. I tried to pat her on the back gently, then located some tissues. I passed them to her until the crying subsided. The feeling of helplessness was truly vile.

Chapter Eighteen

E ventually Martina excused herself to wash her face, and I was left to my thoughts. If these other fae were capable of enslaving these men and forcing them to work, would I be able to get Martine to look around? Surely it was worth a shot, especially as I was in his mind already. After all, the drug was just a conduit for the spell. The alternative was to do nothing but watch and hope he glanced at something that we could identify.

It would be mu magick against theirs.

When Martina came back with her face still damp, I suggested my idea.

'We have nothing left to lose. He feels so tired. He just wants to give up.' She spoke so flatly. Something told me that Martina felt the same.

'I can try, but I need to now keep your emotional reactions out of it. Every time they flare it breaks the connection.' As much as I didn't want to insult her, it was true. While emotions aided the spell, the intensity of what Martina felt was too much for the delicate connection.

'I don't think I can stop that. I just get overwhelmed by it all. The cruelty. Missing him. It's all too much.' She spoke with honesty and integrity, those amber eyes blazing sadly into mine. I sighed.

'There is this old trick I once learned how to do, to essentially wall you off from the work I am doing emotionally. It may be worth it, as you can still witness it, but there won't be the same overwhelming feeling. Did you want to try?' I was careful in my wording, not wanting to spook Martina, nor reveal that it came from my early days of sex work.

She nodded slowly, those big eyes of hers so trusting. I sighed slightly, already starting to feel tired from the magickal exertion. Every time I dipped into his mind it drained my own reserves some more. We needed answers, and I was desperate to see those tears leave Martina's eyes.

This time the dive was much more sluggish, hindered by my fatigue. I slowly built a shimmering barrier around Martina's mind, leaving space only for the anchoring connection between us. Already I could feel the success of the barrier I had built around her psyche. The emotive tension had decreased, and I was free to enter Martine's mind.

Again, I viewed the work through his eyes. I tried to imagine my etheric arms filling his, mimicking his repetitive movements. Soon I became those movements, and I was able to divert his eyes from his task. It happened slowly, but I could look to the left or right of the wall. This offered no further elucidation as to where he was, so I looked further around. Everything was hazy, and I became rapidly frustrated at how hard it was to move in such a reluctant body. All I could feel was a magickal compulsion to continue working. It was an overwhelming desire that I had to try to override to stay in control. Frustration was wearing my nerves thin, however.

Eventually I managed to get his gaze to slide further up, although the effort left me sweating in my own body.

There were warehouses across the way, but rather than the newer, functional ones I had seen when following the previous abductees, these were rusted out shells. Windows were smashed; large holes peppered the tin walls. Many had missing roofs, or their skeletal exposed internal scaffolds lanced the sky.

Others toiled around me, all with their heads down, often with bruises or bloodied limbs and digits. I looked to my left, taking in the oddly shaped building still being built by my captive brethren. It was a mockery of the old temples, full of skewed flourishes and wonky columns.

Hideous statues were being carved, a series of excessively busty women wearing very little was being roughly formed from tree trunks by chainsaw. The carvers were already missing limbs, and at least one had already lost his life and was cast aside, I assumed to be dumped at a more opportune time than the middle of the afternoon.

While I was attempting to memorise every detail and searching for some kind of recognisable feature, the fact that someone had been approaching me had escaped my attention. Before it could register, the man had his arm up and swung his bat. The shock again flung me into my own body, and I was left panting in shock.

While Martina had been protected from fully experiencing what I had, being struck had knocked me loose from her brother's body. I couldn't help but feel a profound guilt. I was sure that he had been hit because of my actions, and felt panicked that I didn't know what happened next.

Trying my hardest to just re-enter my trance from there proved fruitless. I couldn't attain a peaceful state, nor achieve a connection with either twin. Cursing under my breath, I pushed to my feet. That's when I realised how exhausted I was. The room spun around me, my legs gave out, and I fell back to the floor in a sweaty heap. Martina was instantly concerned and moved to my side.

'Jessie! Are you OK? What happened to you? What happened to Martine?' She was frenetic in her apprehension, which was reflected in her voice and static hand movements. I felt dazed and struggled to form a response.

'It worked. I got him to move. I couldn't recognise much, but I got him to move.' I croaked weakly. My throat was raw, it felt as though I had been breathing that dusty air at the compound. I sipped my now cold mug of tea to soothe my throat and my nerves. Feeling my exhaustion, I piled more sugar in to replace some of my energy lost to the ether of spent magick. Martina watched me carefully.

'So, he moved, what does that mean?' The question was well and truly loaded.

'It means that I can override the magick holding him there. For a time being I can take control, but it is exhausting to do so.' I had to be careful in my explanation.

I did not want to get Martina's hopes up only to dash them when I was unable to set him free. Or he was beaten to death because I had moved him.

'Ok, so what made you jump back this time? Did that barrier fail? I tried so hard to keep my emotions in check.' The earnest look in Martina's face was heartbreaking. More heartbreaking was the reason why I was evicted from Martine's mind.

'No, I... there was an incident. I need to get back there fast. I need to change everything. I need more power.' The air around me felt intense and heavy, the room swam as if I was caught in a strongly current of water.

I was hyperventilating.

My sight began to blur.

Martina looked at me with pure concern in her doe eyes. I focused on that, her powerful dignity in the face of all she had lost. Slowing down my breathing was next, as clarity slowly returned to me. Now was not the time to lose it. I needed an excuse.

'Did you mind getting me some water?' My voice croaked dustily as I tried to appease my throat. Could dust stick across etheric leagues or was it simply sympathetic wounds? I was not sure, but I needed Martina out of the room so I could dull my jangling nerves. She nodded and left, and in seconds I had those sweet pills in my hand.

Martina spoke as she was filling a cup.

'Did you see the place he was? It seemed so dry, with so many weird pale bricks. It's hard to believe it would be this century, let alone this city. It looked more like ancient Egypt.' She seemed thoughtful.

'What did you say?' I shouted back, before hurriedly swallowing my pills dry when I heard the tap turn off.

That was not the smartest idea. I choked and spluttered. Martine came back into the room and handed me the water with that knowing grin. I felt such shame.

'I said, it looks more like-.'

With that I remembered what she had said and interrupted her.

'Yes! You know before I got hi- cast back out from him, there was a man dressed very oddly. It was like a skirt. Did you catch what Martine was wearing?' I asked, feeling guilty that I had not looked myself.

'No, only that his arms and probably his chest was bare,' she answered as she took the now empty glass back to the kitchen. I puzzled on the oddness of what I has seen until she returned.

Desperate to re-enter and see the consequences of my actions, I tried to get Martina to settle into the trance again. She insisted on dragging out some heavy ceramic bowl, which annoyed me completely.

'Leave that, we urgently need to get back to Martine, hurry!' I was far too sharp with my orders, and Martina noticed.

'Why, what is of such rush if nothing happened last time?' She managed to be both quiet, but incredibly forceful.

'No such rush, I am just eager to get this over and get some justice, that is all.' The lies rolled out so easily, so easy to spin into a false truth. She looked perplexed, by my answer, but complied.

'What about the herbs Janelle gave you?' The question was careful, tentative. I felt a pang of guilt that Martina felt the need to speak so carefully around me.

'Oh yes!' I exclaimed as I fished them out of my bag. 'Now how to use them. Are they supposed to be a tea?' A feeling of foolishness took my senses as I realised, I had no idea how they were intended to be used.

'No, see this? That is a resin.' Martina pointed out a few odd granules in the blend that I had not noticed. I still looked up blankly. 'Resins are often poisonous for internal consumption. This is an incense blend.' This time she held out her hand for the little pouch of herbs and resin. I handed them over, blushing furiously at my faux pas.

'We burn it?' I asked, blushing harder in shame as Martina emptied the herbs into the ceramic bowl. The mortification I felt was unending. That was why she was obsessing about the bowl, and I was being a jerk. A none too subtle lesson learnt.

Martina lit a piece of charcoal, nestling it under the herbs. In seconds they began to smoke with a beautifully fragrant and somewhat spicy blend. I breathed it in carefully, letting it settle around me. This was certainly a powerful mix. Within seconds I felt like I was floating above my body and saw Martina doing the same. I forced my physical body to settle down, then set to work building the emotion proof wall around Martina. Then I followed the connection to Martine and was there in microseconds.

We walked along an open passageway, with little structure other than rows of columns and a roof. I marvelled at the herbal blend making this so easy. This celebration distracted me from the fact that Martine had stopped dead in his tracks, and someone was shouting at him.

My attention returned however, when both Martine and my etheric body received a blow across the back. I actually felt the pain.

'Defective unit. Move! Needs reprogramming. I hope I can convince the goddesses to just kill this one. It doesn't take well to their magick. Or I can kill it here and tell them it was an accident.' The voice came from behind Martine/ Me, where all the pain was coming from. Whoever it was continued their tirade. 'First, it's looking around, now this. Move damn you. You are going to the goddesses.' That part I took particular notice of.

What goddesses could he possibly mean? There were no deities any more. I realised now that my little incursion into Martine's mind must be total this time, which is why he had stopped walking and why I could still feel the blows currently raining down on my back. I slowly stepped forward. Then another step. It was gloriously easy to do now, compared to last time. I grinned, and the vicious voice behind Martine/ Me got shrill.

'Smiling? This one is fully broken. It needs to be put down. They don't smile.' The voice belonged to a man wearing a ridiculous outfit. Some kind of white skirt, a gold chain and an odd bird shaped club or cane completed this unusual look.

It looked like a cheap Halloween costume, however that club was definitely real. The man himself had just a hint of pink shimmer behind green eyes, indicating at least some control by the spelled drugs. He seemed far more functional than the labouring zombie that was Martine.

I was fast running out of time thanks to my mistakes. It was time to act.

Chapter Nineteen

I looked up ahead of me, seeing two grand doors to a semi-finished building. They were gold coloured, with cats and lotus flowers painted on, made to look like the Egyptian stuff I had seen in history lessons in school. I had barely paid attention to the class, but even I could tell that this was the low rent version.

Suddenly the odd costumes made sense. The pillars, the white bricks, all of it fit together, as bizarre as it was. Whatever was happening, it involved someone's Egyptian fantasy- on a budget.

The shorter man in possession of the shrill voice was really firing up now I was looking around. I took a quick second to say an internal prayer to whoever may be listening and put all my faith into the resilience of Martine's body. It was time to go.

As it arced towards me, the bird club caught my eye, and instinctively I reached out to catch it. As much as the blow hurt my hands, I managed to secure my grasp and wrench the cane from his grip.

His face registered utter shock before I turned the weapon on him. One swift crack to the skull was enough to drop him, but I checked that he was still breathing. He may have been the one beating us and wanting us dead, but there was at least a hint of magickal compulsion there too. It wasn't wholly his fault. I had to believe that.

When I was satisfied that Martine's captor was still alive, I began to look for my escape route. The doors ahead may have these 'goddesses' and some answers behind them, but I really did not want to risk losing Martine now. He was definitely ill equipped to take on a deity.

To my right was the main work area, dust and sweat cloying the air. To the left was a rough attempt at gardens, with lawns constantly being trampled by workers getting more bricks from a storage area in an adjoining warehouse. Clearly the initial site planning had not been well thought out. I pitched left, walking as quickly as possible to the storage warehouse, while still trying to act as though Martine was just doing his job. Inside the warehouse was kept so dim I could barely see a few feet ahead.

As annoying as this was to get orientated with my surroundings, this darkness would cover my escape. I quickly scampered away from the door and crouched down in the shadows to allow my eyes time to adjust.

Dark shapes began to form, and eventually I made out the outline of a door towards the back. Trying to sneak in a hefty male body was unusual, however I managed to creep almost all the way to the door before there was a glint of pink in the dark. A slow voice droned from the gloom.

'Hey, are you supposed to be here?' they drawled, not in full control of their voice or body. I paused, weighing up my options. Luckily this made it seem like my zombie brain was trying to work a reticent body. I tried to match his same tone.

'Yes. Need cement.' I prayed that it worked and I didn't have to beat another victim of this situation. Seconds so long they felt like minutes passed. I held my breath in anticipation. Thankfully there was a shuffling, and the other man walked off into the light without responding. Ironically, he had been holding a bag of cement.

I managed to get to the door without any further interruptions. Finding the handle was hard enough but realising it was locked with a key was a much harder blow. I huffed quietly and again considered my options. Unsure if Martine would even have the strength or weight on him to force open the door, I resolved to try my luck with a very old skill. Moving along the wall lead to a work table, and it was covered in tools and bits of junk. By some blessing I found some scrappy wire pieces, just the right size and strength to pick a lock.

Unlatching the door took no time at all, thanks to my misspent youth. Taking my chances, I cracked the door and peered out. There was a car park, filled with various vehicles. I couldn't see any guards or other people. Of course, I was not trusting that would be the case.

Leaving the door ajar in the hope that someone else would make an escape made me feel a little better. Leaving the hundreds of men that I had seen for the sake of freeing one man felt so wrong to me. This was just the decision I had to make for now.

I made it to the first row of cars without being stopped, and I considered attempting to steal one. Unfortunately, I had no idea how to drive a car. It seemed complicated. Especially while piloting a zombie. I moved through them, checking each one for occupants.

Catching the reflection of Martine/ myself reminded me that he was wearing little more than a loincloth. This ridiculous costume, complete with ankle and wrist manacles would instantly make him/ me recognisable as an escapee.

The first car that I came across with a gym bag got swiftly broken into. I may not steal whole cars, but I certainly knew how to break into them thanks to my hobbies.

Some kind of deity must have been with me, because I managed to find a singlet, shorts and sneakers. I quickly got Martine dressed in the car, nervously checking the surroundings at all times. I re-locked the car and moved on. When I got to the nearest road I walked quickly to the next intersection for the street signs. *Roe and Fifth, Roe and Fifth, Roe and Fifth.* I tried to memorise the roads before attempting to orient myself. With all of my heart, I hoped that I could come back, and hopefully with a good number of Stevie's heavies to clean house.

While I soon figured out a rough location, the path to home was unknown. I resorted to opening the wall between me and Martina in the hopes she could guide me home. I took the chance that she would not overwhelm and collapse the link again. With Martine still under the effect of the fae magick, he may just return to the labour in the compound.

Luckily for all of us, Martina took it wonderfully. She knew which direction to take, and after a few dead ends we managed to get him to more familiar roads. Under her direction, we moved swiftly through the city. There were plenty of stares and nasty comments from passersby, so I figured Martine didn't look too flash.

Soon we were on the home stretch, walking up the street, with the warehouse in sight. I managed to break Martine into a run towards his home, and I could swear that there was a small surge of awareness within him. The magick tying him to the compound had to be weakening. Up until now he had been completely blank, his personality totally suppressed. We were there. The door was before me. A weak knock.

With that the shield collapsed, severing the magickal connection between Martina and myself. What's more, I could feel a small piece of my own magick missing. The hooked segment I had used to anchor me to Martina had been cleanly severed and remained a part of her. Martina had shoved a piece of paper into my hand and bolted to the door. Her eyes were wide with joy. She had accidentally destroyed the shield and severed the link, but I couldn't blame her now.

Squeals erupted from the front door, and tears began to flow. I smiled to myself and looked down at the paper. Roe and Fifth. Somehow Martina had heard and scribbled it down for me. We were gonna get them all out.

Martina dragged Martine into the room, still weeping with joy and pain. Martine looked stunned and no longer had a pink sheen to his eyes. I wasn't sure if it was proximity, my intrusion into his mind or whatever had happened when Martina had severed all the links and barriers, but he was free. Martine was incredibly emaciated, covered in blood and festering sores. He was unable to speak, simply opening and closing his mouth repeatedly.

This once tall black man was now hunched over, limbs like matchsticks ready to break. Even a good portion of his hair had turned grey, in stark contrast to the pictures Martina had showed me. She sat him down on the couch before running into the kitchen to fetch some water. Martine looked at me and began to cry, gingerly touching the softness of the couch with his bruised and bloodied hands.

When Martina returned he ran his fingers down her face, tears falling onto his pilfered clothes. She gripped his hand gently, helping him to sip from the offered cup. Together they cried, touching foreheads in a pure connection. I began to feel uncomfortable, like I was intruding on a personal moment, so I tiredly doused the still burning charcoal and packed up my bag. I rose to sneak out and let them have their reunion. Martina must have seen the movement, because she stopped me on the way to the door.

'I can never repay you for what you have done for me today. But there is so many other men. Whatever little group you are getting to help free them, they can meet in my cafe for a feed and to plan. Just give me some warning. You have done so much, but there is many more to save. For now, I need to get my brother to the hospital and some medical care, but please come and visit me after.' She embraced me and kissed me on the cheek.

Something stirred inside of me; however, I was not about to act upon it during such an emotional time. There was such a genuine glow of joy in her that made me feel it was all worthwhile. I smiled and let myself out of her beautifully industrial front door.

Chapter Twenty

By the time I made it back to the Foxes Den, I was bone tired. I barely waved at Jojo, who appeared to be sporting some new injuries as I dragged myself off to my room. The incense may have given me a power boost, but it had long run out, and I was feeling the after effects of having used so much fae magick. If it was at all possible, I would go to the forest to recharge, but there was no way to do it now.

Instead, I would have to settle for a great long sleep.

As I lay down, I began to type a message to Stevie and Damien to let them know that I knew where all the men were, however I was asleep before I finished the first sentence.

A harsh jangling brought me back to the world of the living. Thankfully I had remembered to plug the phone in this time, and it was now blaring its ringtone in my ear. The little screen showed that Stevie was trying to call, and I groaned as I answered.

'Hrrrrmph... hello Stevie,' I muttered sleepily.

'Jessie. Where are you? Need you in my office now. It's urgent.' With that he hung up. I blinked a few times, trying to process the speed of the phone call. I didn't know what kind of emergency it was, but he certainly sounded upset. I pulled myself out of my bed bound inertia and quickly had a shower. It might be an emergency, but I stank. I dressed quickly in my spare clothes, took my pills and grabbed my bag and keys.

Stevie looked up from his ledgers and papers. A tiredness dogged him, his shoulders slumped and movements limp.

'Jessie, dere is another body. Is Janey's brother. Looks like 'e got 'imself a helluva beat down. All beat an' even all scratched up. Like with 'em fingernails yeah? It ain't good. Janey been chewin' my ear off. She hella mad from findin' me an'... erm, nevah mindin' on that one.' Stevie managed to blush in his grief, and I guessed at the cause.

'You and Liselle huh?' I asked cheekily. I may be pushing my luck, but they seemed like a good match. Stevie could use some legitimacy and wouldn't judge Liselle's past occupation when she graduated. I estimated that they had to be a similar age too.

'Yeah, it be Liselle. We been on a date ye see. Eatin' at a place all fancy like. Only it turns out it belong to Janey's father y'see. He done found out about us and gone tole Janey. She done rushed over an' found 'er brother out by the dumpsters where she be parking. Someone done put 'im there as 'em message.' He looked haggard, aged by this whole affair, as opposed to his usual neutral facade. Even his toughness had faded. A feeling of dread settled over me as I saw the effect it was having on him. Right now, we needed his power, his guile. Whatever was killing these men would need to be stopped with his influence. I shivered slightly, having seen how many people were at the compound.

'Stevie, I am so sorry. But I know where they are. I got one of the men out already, and we can go back for the rest. I feel like this is my fault though, because I got Martine out, they took it out on him. That's just twisted. How did they know to take him there?' I mused, as Stevie listened intently.

'So, you knowin' where ter go? We can get 'em done and all ovah?' He finally allowed a small smile to break through. I returned in kind.

'Yeah. Corner of Roe and Fifth in the industrial part of deep South Bayton. There is a warehouse and some kind of temple. I saw it all through his eyes,' I said proudly. There was always a small part of me that constantly feared that Stevie would arbitrarily decide that I was not working hard enough and kick me back into the street.

It was rooted in my own pride, but also the need to keep living off the streets. I had gotten too used to my little slice of luxury.

'So ye got him, but how ye havin' the stuff to save him, but not 'em others? What makin' him so special?' he asked without any hint of malice.

'He was the one with a twin sister. I could use faery magick to create a link between them and control him. But there was so many men there Stevie. I figured there had to be well over a hundred there. It was really bad. But at least I know a way we might be able to get in. I just need manpower. They have guards with weird club things, and who knows what else.' Everything came out in a big jumble thanks to my mixed-up senses of both excitement and trepidation. I didn't want to risk any more men, but there was no way I was getting in without them.

Stevie nodded sagely. 'I will see who Jojo can rustle up. What's next?'

'Well, I need to see if there are any details I can get from Martine that may be useful. There is also a place we can all meet beforehand. I need to talk to Damien too, see if he can supply some men. Nathaniel can get fucked.' With my final comment Stevie roared with laughter. A haughty voice whined from the doorway.

'I think it is highly inappropriate to be laughing in such a manner right now Steven.' Stevie's mirth fled as he looked to the person standing in the doorway behind me. I groaned quietly and turned to face Janey.

'Hello Janey, I am so sorry for your loss.' I tried to sound as sincere as possible.

'You ought to be sorry, your pathetic work is why he is dead. He died because of you. Incompetent bitch.' She spat at me, looming over my chair. The shrew needed to fully bend over to get right up in my face. I blinked slowly, once, twice. Initially I was of a mind to punch her then and there, but I held back, reminding myself that she had just lost a loved one.

'I understand that you have just lost someone dear to you, but it was only today that we managed to locate the compound. Prior to that it was kept too hidden, with plenty of guards in the surrounding streets for quite a distance.' I explained calmly, thankful for my pills numbing my reactions and emotions. All class, Janey snorted loudly.

'Piss-weak excuses, you are all useless. Guards and bullshit. I thought you were supposed to be all powerful?' The glare of the shrew turned to Stevie in an instant, and I was happy for the distraction.

'Welp, guess I better go coordinate the rescue party. Will message you later with times Stevie.' I yelled over my shoulder as I bolted out the door. I swear I heard a whimper from him as I left them alone in the room. Poor Stevie. I almost felt sorry for him. Almost.

As I left the front entrance, I heard a familiar sassy voice call my name. Smiling, I turned to Liselle and Sadie.

'I am so glad you are here; I was going to contact you to let you know that Martine is free!'

'We knowin' that. That pretty sister of his actually be callin' Sadie to tell her. Be just comin' from there now, him's hospital. He gonna be OK cos of yer work.' Lisette spoke up. Sadie started frantically signing to both of us. 'Aw yeah, Sadie sayin' thank ye. When Martine woke up, he done proposed to her. They gonna get clean an' get married. Ye saved her future husband now. He done got inspired ter get offa the drugs fer them to live a good life.' She translated with a beaming smile. After the tense accusations from Janey, this was too much. I broke down and ugly cried. A future. A marriage. I had saved someone. The ladies gathered around me in a tissue sharing embrace.

'I'm sorry. I am so happy for you. It's just been a hell of a day so far. I promise I am so happy for you.' I blubbered as they tried to soothe me. 'I have to go organise a force to start a rescue. There is so many men, and they are all mentally enslaved. There are guards... now I need to convince people it's worth fighting for them but not hurting them. I don't know what to do, but I gotta do it.'

'Ye needin' help? Ok, ye tell me a time and place and Imma have people fer ye. Sendin' me a message yeah?' Liselle said firmly. I nodded as I cleaned up my face with a shredded tissue. 'Now Imma go see... Um... well Imma see Stevie about some stuff.' She said awkwardly.

I giggled wetly.

'I know about you and Stevie. But don't go in there now, his ex-wife is there. She is not happy.' Now it was time for Liselle to snort with laughter.

'Aye, Janey be a real piece o' work. She done tried ter fight me, an' I was just eatin' dinner. That's a nasty lady that one. Thanks, fer the warning, me an' Sadie gonna hang back then.' She nodded and signed an explanation to Sadie. They both nodded and disappeared off into the crowd.

This day was an emotional roller coaster, and dusk had barely tainted the sky.

On the walk over to Bayton Central I called Martina. I had to see how she was doing, and Martine of course. I tried to tell myself it was to check in on Martine, even though Liselle had just talked to me about it.

'Hello Jessie, our hero!' Martina answered happily.

'Hi Martina. How is Martine feeling?'

'He is doing so well. He is severely underweight and has to have IV antibiotics for all the infected sores, but he is going to make a full recovery.' Her voice conveyed just how ecstatic she was about the outcome. It made me smile just to hear it. 'He is even going to go to meetings, get clean and all.'

'Yeah, Sadie told me that just now.' I responded happily.

'Did she tell you that he proposed? I had no idea that they were so serious. But I am thrilled for him. I think this whole situation really scared him and put things into perspective.'

'Yeah she did. Sadie was so happy she was crying. But I have to ask, did Martine remember anything about the weird temple thing or what happened there? I am trying to organise a... well a rescue or whatever.' Any little tidbit may seriously help our chances.

'No, he doesn't remember a single thing up until he was at our door. Everything else is just blank. Partial amnesia, the doctor said. He can remember the past, but nothing since he took fizz as he called it.' Martina sounded dejected as she explained the situation. I couldn't help but mirror that feeling.

'Ok. I spoke to Stevie and am on my way to see Damien. I will let you know when we are all gonna meet up. I gotta go, I am almost there.'

'Ok. Hey Jessie? Thank you again. I really hope I can repay you some day.' Martina was so earnest before she hung up that I felt close to tears again.

Chapter Twenty-One

When I got to the night market, they told me that Damien was doing his rounds with Luis. I sat and waited for a few minutes before I remembered that I had a phone to be able to call him. The call went through almost immediately.

'Eh Jessie. What ye be needin'?' He spoke carefully; there must have been too many ears around.

'I found out where the compound is with the missing men. Can I talk to you? I'm outside your office.'

'Ye, I be up on der top level of de market. Ye kin find me there. See ye soon.' He abruptly hung up. I wondered if I had upset him somehow.

The stairs were easy enough to find, but the crowd on the upper level of the market was packed tight. I had to elbow my way through, desperately jumping up to see over the sea of heads.

The fae were usually very short, and not even my half human side could save me from that. I made it to a break in the crowd, and ostensibly Damien was at its centre. People liked him, but the body guard Luis kept them at arm's length unless they were actively talking to him. That offered about as much privacy as was possible in such a situation.

'Hi Damien. So, I found where...' I stopped as he held a hand up.

'Not here Jessie. We gotta see someone up 'ere, den we can be talkin' bout it. C'mere.' He beckoned, and I followed. We wove towards the nearest stall, where a middle-aged man gloomily sold his wares. When Damien approached he nodded. Tears fell from his eyes.

'This 'ere be Jessie. She de one who found about 'em bad drugs. She de one who gonna be savin' all dem others.' He spoke quietly to the man while Luis pushed people out of earshot of the whisper. The man nodded, his creased face now harsh with wrath.

'Get 'em revenge for me on who that done it. They done killed my boy. Ye be stoppin' this for me.' The man said, his accent somewhere between the usual Bayton lingo and something more exotic. I nodded, unable to trust my voice. Damien stepped in for me.

'Ye know I was always gonna get a good revenge fer ye boy, Marcus. We gonna make sure ain't no one get away that did this. I promise ye that.' With that the men nodded, and Damien turned back to me. 'Let's get inside. Can talk more.' Luis instantly began to move the crowd, so we could slip through unimpeded.

I followed Damien dutifully, trying to ignore the fact that he smelt good, even in the crush of sweaty and often dishevelled people around us.

When we were spirited away to the privacy of his office Damien first offered me a drink, then indicated me to give the details.

'I know where the place is that the men are being held. I got one of them out, but he doesn't remember anything about being there. But I saw the nearest intersection.' I pulled out the piece of paper that Martina had written on to remind me. 'It's Roe and Fifth, in an area with a bunch of warehouses. Deep South Bayton.' As I spoke Damien pulled out a tablet computer. In seconds he had the intersection marked on a map. He cursed softly.

'Aye, I be knowin' this part. All this suppose to be poison land. 'Em warehouses all abandoned. Big industrial spill got all dese blocks closed off 'ere.' He encircled a huge chunk of map, with the intersection of Roe and Fifth right in the centre. 'Ain't no one go dere, cos of it bein' so deadly. Been 'bout 5 years now. Even de water ain't good. Gone in de water tunnels,' he explained. I whistled quietly in awe.

'That bad huh? Will it be safe enough to go in there?' My voice trembled with nervous energy. The last thing I wanted to do was endanger more people while trying to save the others.

'Aye am sure we kin get 'round it. We just don't be spendin' long dere or drinkin' no water.'

'Ok. Can you help with this? Any men want to help? There is hundreds of men there, and I am not sure how to stop them. They are innocent puppets.' I was desperate to not lose any more men on my watch.

'How can we be tellin' if they be a puppet or de master?' Damien certainly had an eye for important details that even I missed, and this was supposed to be my investigation.

'I know that so far all the affected men have a pink glitter to their eyes. I am just guessing that whoever casts and controls this magick doesn't, as it is not a normal faery trait. They would have an eye sheen like mine. I think the glitter is a sign of the magick active in them. That and they will probably be women. Short women,' I explained, hoping with all my heart that I was right. As much as I didn't want an innocent man punished, I did not want the culprits to get away either. They could always start up whatever this devilry was again.

'Ok, so we be tryin' ter free de ones with pink in dem eyes. Will tell me boys. When ye plannin' on doin' dis?' He spoke without a hint of doubt about me in his voice. His faith in me was humbling.

'Well, I gotta get everyone together first. Stevie will bring some muscle and even Liselle is getting involved. We are gonna meet at Maydwell's Urban Grind. But what time do you think would be the best for this?' I was hoping to benefit from his expertise.

'Well, used to be dis kinda shebang was done at night. But Imma guessin' daytime'd be better, so me boys can see 'em difference with dey eyes. Don't want no one gettin' away neither. But 'em sun gone down now, so ain't no good till t'morrow,' he said with a glance at his watch. In this windowless room I was surprised that he knew night had fully fallen. I guessed it made sense for someone who had a trade that ran under the cover of darkness. It was literally his business to know.

'Ok, so we do it tomorrow. Meet you at Maydwell's Urban Grind at noon?' I made the request tentatively. I was still half expecting the return of the first Damien I had met, the surly one who completely disrespected me and other "users". I expected him to tell me to do it by myself.

'Aye sounds good. Will bring who I can. Ye working tonight?' His voice softened with that question.

'No, I need to rest after using so much magick to get Martine out. I expect I will need a lot more for tomorrow too. I will just sleep instead,' I responded, confused by him making it sound like a personal question.

'Ah, yeah. Dat be makin' sense,' he muttered. Sensing the weird awkwardness in the room, I stood to leave. 'Hey Jessie, ye be seein' anyone right now?'

I was stunned.

'No, but I have feelings for someone. I'm not very good at dating one person though. Most of the fae are polyamorous,' I explained gently. It was clear he was asking for a reason, and I didn't want to hurt him like the last person had.

'Poly what now?' he queried, adorably confused.

'Polyamorous. It means we date multiple people at the same time, with their permission of course. Everyone has to consent to it.'

'Aye, dat be interestin' fer sure. Glad ye be open bout dis. I be respectin' dat.' He nodded abruptly, summarily ending the conversation. But it wasn't in anger or derision. There was something comfortable in it. I said my goodbyes and left.

A quick text to Liselle, Martina and Stevie while I walked home, and everything was set. I hit my pillow with nervous butterflies causing hurricanes in my gut, but eventually I fell into a restless sleep.

Chapter Twenty-Two

I woke early, to begin to centre my magick and focus on what the day would bring. I even did some stretches, anticipating that the day would be pretty strenuous. Showering took longer than usual as I pondered my options and took the time to scrub everything. For clothing I opted for older items, not willing to let my new things get ruined.

Phone fully charged, holding precious confirmation messages that each faction would be there today, I tucked it into my bag beside my knife. There was a definite vibe of a warrior preparing for battle. Pulling on my boots and taking some extra pills for energy was my final tasks, and I stepped out of my door.

Planning to get some breakfast at Maydwell's Urban Grind, I walked over an hour earlier than I had asked the others to be there. Martina was back behind the coffee machine, that infectious smile back on her face.

'Jessie, you are early my dear! What would you like?' she called out. My stomach did little irritating flutters when she looked at me, or spoke, or did anything really.

'Can I get a coffee and one of them amazing burgers?' I asked as I fished out some money.

'Darlin, you never have to pay here again. Don't you try it.' Her smile was glorious, the warmth of her sincere joy and pure beauty giving my life sunlight. A thousand romantic lines flittered through my head. My sun, my moon, and all the stars in the sky. The light of my life, my heart. Blessed sunshine after the storm.

Instead, I coughed awkwardly and nodded.

Resigned to my failure, I crept over to a booth to hide my shame.

'Aww, you remembered,' Martina gushed when she brought my coffee over.

'Wha?' I asked, totally confused.

'This was the booth we sat at when we first met.' Martina answered with her husky laugh. I tensed, unsure if I had been accidentally romantic or just a platonically cute memory. The butterflies in my stomach just died of shock.

'I... uh... yes, it's very s-special to me.' Lawd, now I was stuttering. Would the mortification never end? One beautiful woman and I was a mess. But Martina wasn't just a beautiful woman. She was so much more than that and that is the part that got me all flustered. I realised that I had lost myself staring into the coffee when Martina had to call my name multiple times. 'I'm sorry, I was distracted, what did you say?'

'I was just thanking you for the ten millionth time for saving my brother. He has really changed his life around after such a traumatic event. They won't release him from the hospital yet but just know how grateful he is. I was hoping, after all of this was over, that I could take you out to dinner... to say thank you of course!' Martina blurted out the last part so rapidly that I finally noticed her awkwardness.

I couldn't help but do a little happy dance. She giggled also, and we broke into peals of laughter just as Janelle delivered my burger. A small queue was starting to build up, so Martina had to return to her customers.

I had the time to eat my burger in peace as I pondered what this day would entail. While I had gathered some assorted muscle from Stevie and Damien, I wasn't really sure how to deal with the magickal side of things. While I knew it was faerie magick, I still knew nothing of the casters, the intricacies of the spell or the way to unravel it. I was just kind of hoping that it would be obvious when I got there, but I was very dubious of my own skills.

I could weave a wicked hallucination, but anything more advanced would be beyond me. After the death of my mother, my paternal grandparents had essentially thrown me into a mundane school and life as a whole.

The little bell on the cafe door rang frantically as Stevie entered, followed by ten burly, beardy beast men. Soon after Damien came in, followed by at least 15 strong men, all terribly attempting to conceal some type of weapon. They were all soon sizing each other up as Damien and Stevie approached me, sliding into the booth awkwardly.

'Aye, we got 'em men, all 'em good fighters. De best.' Damien puffed himself up in pride. Not to be outdone, Stevie soon joined in.

'Got some of me best guards fer ye Jessie. They gonna be able to get through anything we need to. All be mighty powerful,' Stevie crowed, looking at his men with pride. I had never before seen something so foolish. Two men measuring dicks while on a rescue mission. I snorted and finished my food.

'Well, we here, and ye be done eatin'. I reckon 's 'bout time we get goin'. Get dis done with and all,' murmured Damien as he moved to stand up.

"Not yet, I am still waiting on someone else who was going to help,' I muttered back, sipping my coffee. Both men groaned loudly.

'You brought Nathaniel in? I thought ye wasn't gonna get him involved. He ain't never do nothin' fer free too. You gonna owe him even if ye helpin' him too.' Stevie warned me.

'Nope, it's definitely not Nathaniel. Ooh here she is now!' I said happily. Both men looked confused.

'She?' They queried almost in unison. Liselle entered, followed by Sadie and a gaggle of street girls. There had to be close to 35 women all gathered together. Rather than size each other up like the men, they all gathered around the cake fridge, excitedly enquiring if they could buy a whole cake to split it.

Liselle and Sadie came to join the rest of the leaders. Stevie looked shocked.

'Liselle, ye shouldn't be here, it's not safe. I can't protect all of ye girls and deal with this. Send 'em home.'

Now Liselle looked absolutely mulish.

'One, most of these ladies don't have homes to go to. Two, we are all perfectly capable of looking after ourselves. Three, I ain't doin' what ye say anyways.' Damien burst into laughter, but stifled it quickly at a sharp, withering look from Liselle.

A cheer broke out as the girls got their cake. They refused a set of individual plates, instead grabbing a fork each and carrying the whole cake to a table. It was demolished in seconds. The men stood around the edges of the room looking shocked. There was a regular whisper of words like hooker, prostitute or sluts.

'Aye Jessie. These girls gonna distract me boys. Ain't enough men to protect them all,' whispered Stevie. Liselle signed angrily to Sadie, and both looked absolutely mutinous.

'My *women* aren't here for protection. Many lost boyfriends or clients and they want their revenge. They are all streetwise and smarter than the gaggle of muscles you two brought. These are the ladies who practice self-defence on the side and can pack a mean punch. If your *boys* can't stop themselves from being distracted, they aren't particularly good guards or whatever they are supposed to be.' Liselle's retort slapped Stevie in the face, and he sat looking stunned. I was impressed. Damien was smart and kept his mouth shut.

'Glad to have you along Liselle. They make quite the army.' I gave her a wicked smile, enjoying that two 'tough' men just got silenced by this goddess of a woman. I grabbed a pen and my notebook out of my bag. 'Now, this is a rough idea of what the compound looks like. I got Martine out through a door here. As far as I could tell, all guards and workers are under the spell. So, we have to make sure we do not injure them too much. A rescue is no good if they are dying in the meantime.

This is the big closed off building where they were taking Martine to meet the "goddesses". I think whoever started all this will be holed up in here. We gotta make sure that they don't get away. I bet they would just keep going. They seem pretty dangerous. So, we have to try and intercept any exits, OK?' I finished up cautiously. When I realised that everyone had stopped to listen to me, I was shocked. They were all looking at me. People started nodding slowly.

'Aye Jessie. We gon' do it how ye want it done. Ye be leadin' dis,' Damien answered reverently. This all felt very disconcerting. I had no business leading anyone. I was only doing this to get off the streets for a bit. Well and to make Martina happy. But here they all were, competing gang leaders, their soldiers and a whole flock of street ladies. All listening to me.

Shit.

The very idea had bile rising in my throat.

Liselle was the next to brave speaking.

'Ya hear that girls? No killing them, no escapees. Let's get this done!' A chorus of agreement rang out, and people began to file out of the front door. I was left both shocked and amused. This felt like madness, but there was no going back now.

The walk to the industrial area was interesting to say the least. Despite having disrespected them earlier, many of the men tried to proposition the women, only to be soundly rejected. They were intent on freeing the men affected and they were all hopped up on chocolate cake.

There was no stopping these women now, no distractions. Several others joined us on the march, called over by friends or gawking and having the cause explained to them. By the time they made it to the corner of Roe and Fifth, their numbers had swollen to almost 50 various street people.

Stopping before we entered the parking lot, I pointed to the door set into the side.

'That's where I got Martine out. It leads straight into the whole central area. I left it unlocked, but I doubt it still will be,' I explained in a rough whisper.

'Leave that to us!' Grunted the largest ones in the group of men, all puffing out their chests with a sincere but conceited bravado.

'No, wait!' I interjected, too late.

With that, all Hel broke loose. The manly men, in an effort to show off to the women they had once called sluts, promptly ran over to the door. They began throwing themselves at it, kicking and hurling their entire bodies into it. Suddenly they stopped, looking confused. The ones who stood further back began to jeer at the stunned ones. In seconds a fight broke out.

Liselle looked at me with a disapproving jerk of her head towards the men. They were beginning to knock each other out. Stevie rubbed a hand over his skull stubble.

'What got inter 'em?' He was clearly miffed. 'Them's two is brothers. Zachie, Kyle, get in there and separate 'em. Damned fools.'

Zachie and Kyle, two of the smaller brutes that came along with Stevie marched over. Damien nodded at a few of his men that had held back. They strode over as yet another man was knocked out. While there was an attempt made to separate the men, one of Damien's men and Zachie decided to try their luck with the door. They at least decided to coordinate their attacks, kicking together a few times before they too stopped suddenly.

I couldn't help but groan into my hand.

'Guys... the door opens out. And... yep, they are falling under the spell,' I pointed out as Zachie and Brutus-whatever-his-name-was turned on their fellow men fighting in front of the door.

Soon they wiped out those who were left and came at the rest of us, pink eyes glimmering in the sunlight as they got closer. Liselle snorted with laughter and stepped forward with the rest of her crew. A few swift hits and kicks later, the entranced men dropped.

'Ready to do this Jessie?'

'I've got my wire,' I responded, holding up my little makeshift lockpicking kit. 'You lot stay back here before you donate any more guards to their cause.'

'Ye can't be goin' in without protection!' exclaimed Stevie, with agreeing nods from his few remaining men.

'One, those women handled your big brawny men just fine. Two, your men couldn't even get through the door. Oh, and three, most women seem immune to the drug and spell.' I didn't wait for an answer, instead trotting over to the door.

Liselle signed quickly to Sadie, who then signed something obscene to the men, and joined me at the door. We moved as quietly as possible, given that I wasn't really sure if someone on the other side was directing the spell, or if it just worked via proximity.

I pulled the wires I had kept out of my bag, checking first if the door was even locked. I didn't trust the first lot of men to have actually checked the door prior to attempting to batter it down. To their credit, it was at least locked.

My wires worked a treat, and I soon had that barrel turning. Before opening the door, I looked back to my all-female squad of rescuers. I nodded, they nodded and we were in.

The warehouse was darker than I remembered, and I soon realised why. The larger door to the inside of the compound was shut. I checked for any telltale eye glitters before creeping across to where I remembered the door to be. It took a few attempts, but I finally found the opening.

'Shit, I think they actually locked this door or something. If only I had a light.' I mused thoughtfully, trying to remember if I had seen a flashlight around. The room was bathed in light as around 10 women drew out their mobile phones and put their torches on.

I cursed softly as I realised they had chained the sliding door closed, with a padlock securely fastened on the other side. There was no way I could access the lock to pick it. We were stymied again.

'If only I had thought to bring a bolt cutter or something. We could have done this by now...' I ran my fingers through my faerylocks.

'We got it,' piped up one of the older ladies, stepping out of the shadows wielding an angle grinder. Her maniacal grin combined with her long black hair and love for fishnet clothing made for an impressive view. She gunned it, the screech bellowing out through the warehouse. With a gleeful laugh she cut through the chain effortlessly, followed by cutting her initials into the door.

We had a giggle, then the angle grinder was thrown aside, and we collectively slid the stubborn door open. So far none of the girls, nor myself had succumbed to the spell. I hazarded a guess that same sex interests alone were not enough to trigger infatuation.

When the door was wide enough for us to flood out we came face to face with a group of their guards. They all wore the white skirt thing and bore the bird shaped clubs. Behind them a lone figure in a flowy gown stamped their foot and ran to the pillared walkway.

'Leave... now... and... we... will... spare... you.' The men all chanted in unison, their mouths not their own. I smirked. No chance.

'Sorry, we don't make deals with the devil, or in this case, puffed up pseudo goddesses.'

'How... did... she... know? Who... cares... kill... her,' the men repeated.

I took note of that little nuance. Was there more than one person responsible for all of this? There wasn't long to ponder on that thought as the men rushed us as one.

'Don't forget, these men are being controlled. Don't kill 'em,' I shouted to the others. The one with a love of fishnets kicked one of the more bedraggled men in the side of his head, a perfect roundhouse kick.

'I know, that's me husband,' she yelled back, pointing at the prone man. I was shocked but giggled regardless.

Duck, weave, punch, duck, kick. Rinse and repeat. We had the men all unconscious or otherwise incapacitated in a few minutes of scuffling. Some of the women had taken a blow or two, but overall, they were in far better shape.

I organised for the girls to spread out around the temple, in the hope that we could prevent anyone leaving. When only one other exit door was found, I stationed three of the toughest ladies there in order to intercept any escapees. I took Liselle, and by extension Sadie, to the main door.

It was exactly as ornate as I remembered, full of colour and gold paint. There was a definite Roman flair, although it was filtered through the minds of the deranged people who had orchestrated this mess and their pet zombies. The result was a poor imitation, blended with the other Egyptian decor. Still, the doors were large and seemed fairly solid. I pressed my whole body against them, but they did not budge.

Sadie started to sign to Liselle, who excitedly translated.

'What if we used a smacking... beating... oh battering ram!'

'Actually, that may just work,' I answered with a distracted mutter as I immediately began to look around for a suitable item. Two of the nearby women looked around, finding a pillar that had fallen. They seemed delighted to find out that the core was just a wooden pylon. Soon the rest of the ladies dug some rope out of the workshops. These remarkably resourceful women had soon turned a blank pylon into a serviceable battering ram, and we were lining it up.

With five girls on each side and two of our biggest securing the end, we ran at the door with a war cry. The battering ram hit the door and then went straight through. The door didn't open, oh no. It burst straight through two thin layers of wood, punching a hole right in the gut of it.

The girls looked at the ram, looked at the door and promptly dropped the battering ram. They began to tear it apart with a banshee wail, kicking it out and ripping the pieces off that they could. This mighty, decorated door was destroyed in no time by a group of pissed off sex workers.

We stepped through the rubble to confront another group of men, this time at least one had a handgun. We watched warily, shifting our weight, preparing for the attack. Any weapon we had was now brandished openly. It was a tense standoff.

'Leave... us... alone. Go... away.' The chorus of men struggled to speak in their stupor. These had clearly been most of the labourers, all emaciated, covered in white dust and sores. More interestingly was the fact that the men were echoing a whiny voice from the back of the room. A second voice also spoke, this one sounding much more confident.

'Leave... the... temple... of... the... almighty... goddesses... before... they... smite... you.' I smiled in response, damned sure that whatever beings were at the back of this hokey temple, they were not goddesses. I shrugged.

'Hmmm... nope!' Without waiting for my words to register, I ran at one of the men with a handgun. I spear tackled him and we both went down hard. Luckily his head landed on the foot of another man, rather than the concrete floor. It was still enough to knock him out cold.

I grabbed the gun from him as another of the zombie army brought a large plank of wood down on my head. I collapsed onto the man I had tackled. The fighting continued around me as my world whirled. Unconsciousness threatened, but I managed to hold on. Slowly I got up, turned and punched a man who was grappling with a short blonde girl. He dropped like a rock, and we continued working our way through the crowd.

There had to be at least 35 men, but my Amazons were making short work of them. When I spotted a gap in the fighting I made a break for it. I ran around a small pool of water, unwilling to get my relatively new boots wet and risk ruining them. There was a sort of stone stage, and on top stood three honest to goodness thrones.

In each sat a full blood faerie, slightly shimmering in the sunlight as their magick soaked the air. A snake coiled through the thrones in an idle slither, its eyes also glittering pink. If I could hazard a guess, it was some sort of python, large but not venomous.

'Begone or I shall smite you where you stand.' Growled the red haired one to the left side. Her voice was oddly musical, for all the hate dripping from her words. I groaned audibly when I realised what they were.

Musical voices and a blue pallor to their skin was classic of the sirens. Plus, their eyes shimmered pink, which was a fact I did not know. Sirens were generally pretty, arrogant and irresistible to all who were ensnared by their magick. Men were particularly susceptible. Contrary to the old tales it was not their voices alone that worked to create willing slaves, but a general aura.

'Ugh, sirens. The laziest of all the fae.' I spoke loud enough for them to hear even on their ridiculous thrones. Their neutral faces quickly contorted into pure rage.

'How dare you. We are each part of a triple goddess. Our devotees work to build the temple we deserve, one that we will change the disgusting state of the world with.' The central one with black hair spoke with a surprising amount of control. She seemed much surer of herself than the redhead.

The third, a grey-haired siren, had stayed silent for the entirety of the process. They were all dressed in very sheer and floaty costumes, with a rather Greek style, but entirely modern fabrics. There was a pretty shimmer to the chiffon as it clung to every curve, wrapping sensuously around limbs. The look was finished with gold-coloured Roman sandals. They really did look a lot like triplets, although that could just be the costumes.

The other girls joined me, warily looking at each of the sirens. Some of the girls had to support each other to walk, and more than one was actively bleeding, but we had done well enough.

'Good grief, you nutbags. This is all nothing more than one giant cultural appropriation. You had Egyptian workers, Greek pillars, a Roman door and now you are pretending to be a Celtic triple goddess? You all even dyed your hair to fit this fantasy.' I spluttered with the rage of a child obsessed with ancient civilisations as a means of escapism.

'Well, aren't you so much cleverer than those around you?' The grey-haired one finally spoke. Unlike the other two, her voice was much huskier. I could see why she would choose to emulate the crone.

'Sure. And I gotcha, so how about stopping that little siren spell you have going on in the drugs?' I asked optimistically. I didn't really expect it to work, but I needed to delay a little to see if there was a way to destroy the link they had with the men. I desperately felt around metaphysically, searching for any tendrils of a magickal link. So distracted by the search, I missed the next thing the sirens said. It was only when one of my girls responded that I paid attention.

'I don' be carin' what bullshit ye be spinnin'. I want me brother and me boyfriend back now or we gonna have troubles,' shouted a feisty woman with short red hair that really reminded me of the stereotypical pixie. Her serious curves and stubborn stance really cemented the image. I tried my hardest not to laugh aloud. It turned out that I should not have worried as the three sirens all burst out into laughter.

'We are goddesses. You dare to threaten us?' blurted out the maiden one, her curly red hair bouncing with each peal of laughter. By this time my patience had worn thin. There was no existing links to the men, so the answer had to lie in these brain addled fae. I felt a prickle of magick nosing around but could not really place it.

Exasperated, I just pulled out the gun I had taken from the bad guys, levelling it at the central siren. It felt a lot heavier than I ever thought a gun could, but thanks to some of the movies I had watched, I knew to take the safety off. The siren looked shocked.

'Just release them all. I am sick of dodging around everything. Let the men go or I do this the old-fashioned way. Shoot first and ask questions later.' Some of the other girls followed suit, putting up pilfered hand guns. The little redhead scooted over to a prone body and grabbed one she must have forgotten about.

Definitely pixie blood in her.

The feeling of nosing magick disappeared. The dark-haired siren put her hands up and started to talk suspiciously loudly. I didn't notice her words at all though, I was too busy watching the grey-haired siren start to mutter. Movement out of the corner of my eye made my attention jump across.

One of the girls who had a gun was slowly turning, aiming at me. I pointed the gun at the grey siren, shouting at her to stop, but she never responded. Looking at the girl, I realised she was tensing to shoot. With my heart in my throat and pulse pounding in my ears, I fired. What I had intended to be a low, maybe a kneecap shot, went high as the gun kicked back. The resultant shot hit the centre of her chest. She slumped over in the throne, likely dead already.

The girl with her gun pointed at me dropped it on the floor in shock. We all followed suit, unwilling to become pawns for the enemy. The remaining two sirens stood shocked. We all had ringing ears and a horrible feeling, well I did at least. Despite my burgeoning guilt, it was confirmed, one way to break the spell was death of the siren.

All was silent for untold seconds. The drip of blood was audible from the siren I had shot before even knowing her name.

A guttural, wordless screech came from the middle siren, her black hair trailing behind her as she threw herself towards us.

The redhead also stood but instead chose to run behind the wall the thrones were set against.

'Wait, don't do this!' I desperately shouted at the teary siren as she scooped up one of the dropped guns. As she was trying to work the safety, Liselle stepped forward and punched her right in the forehead. The siren dropped straight down, collapsing to the concrete. She was surrounded by a halo of chiffon and glitter.

I was awed by the epic swing that Liselle wielded. Liselle and Sadie then secured the siren by sitting on her, while I was reminded that there was still one more siren. I beckoned at fishnets and the pixie, and we slowly peeked around the wall. There was no one there, although the room behind the thrones appeared to be a very messy dressing room. All kinds of costumes lay all over the place, along with street clothes.

Mirrors lined the wall, and they all had great offerings of cosmetics before them. Glitters, bronzers, powders and pencils were everywhere. The floor was absolutely coated in shoes, of more types and designs than I ever knew existed. I kicked them out of the way, unwilling to now break my ankle on a wayward heel.

'Over dere, bein' a way out.' The pixie pointed to a sort of hallway that joined the back of the room. There also appeared to be a walk-in closet adjoining the room, which was definitely surprising. This whole room seemed to be used as a closet, a second seemed superfluous.

'You two keep an eye on this hallway while I check the closet. Don't forget that she might have a weapon,' I ordered them, snapping at first, then trying to soften my words. They moved to the mouth of the hallway, and I went to the closet.

I actually had to check that she wasn't hiding under the mountain of clothes on the floor. This was all so foreign to me. The luxury of so many clothes seemed bizarre in my world of poverty. Convinced that she wasn't hiding there, I returned to the hallway. We found a filthy kitchenette, pantry, an equally disgusting bathroom and finally a bedroom.

Clearly the sirens had not shared any of these facilities with the men. All of this mayhem was done by them.

It was when we headed to the very back of the temple that we finally found her. Well, more specifically, the women I had asked to guard the back door did. They dragged her in, an ornate knife sticking out of her abdomen.

'We din' do it. She done 'ad a knife an' gon' stab us, then she done stab 'erself.' One of the girls earnestly tried to justify the wounding as if I would be angry at them. I got them to lay her on a bed, but it was too late. She was already gone.

Sighing loudly, I went to the bathroom to wash the blood off my hands. While there I also took my chance to take some extra pills. My nerves were shot and I was trembling. While I had done plenty of bad things in life, I had never killed anyone. Now I had shot one person and been responsible for the death of many. With that thought I promptly vomited.

Chapter Twenty-Three

I had cleaned myself up feverishly, needing to rejoin the other girls. We still had to check the rest of the compound to find the other trapped men and be sure that there was not a fourth siren hidden away. We couldn't assume that the spell was broken now that two of the sirens were dead. Assuming anything had gotten my ass into hot water enough times this week alone.

Coming out of the temple, we finally braved the construction side. It was even more shocking in person. We found another four dead men, all beaten or starved to death. Other than the corpses, there wasn't a single man in sight. We could see many walls being built, all linking together in some kind of labyrinth, but a quick climb on top of one wall revealed it to be empty.

Behind the maze was a low building, made with rough bricks and cheap sheets of tin. They were rusted and bent, messily making up something resembling a roof. It was in this building that I finally found more of the men, all cowering in the dusty gloom. This seemed to be where the workers slept. Dirty blankets lay on the bare floor, and buckets lined the back wall, filled to overflowing with human waste. The stench was overwhelming.

The men themselves were thin and absolutely filthy. Once again many had open sores which were actively rotting, oozing down dirt caked skin. Quite a few had broken bones, especially fingers and toes. I set to work trying to question them for any information with the other women.

The beaten men were all alert, although very confused about personal orientation. I left some of the women there, including the pixie, who had found her brother. Under the dirt, he had the exact same shock of red hair as his sister.

They cried and hugged enthusiastically. My heart ached a little at their closeness. The rest of us continued our search.

Towards the very back of the complex there was a warehouse with two opposing entry doors. One was locked, so we tried the other first. Inside were the rest of the men. They must have run here after coming to lucidity, many still clutching tools and covered in concrete. None bore the sheen of the spell, which relaxed the tension in me considerably.

No other siren was to be found there, so we sent the new group of men to go wait with the others. In all we had to have found at least 75 men so far. Some were fresh, taken in the latest groups I had seen. Many were less fortunate; their skin reduced to shreds of flesh over pustules and necrosis. They shuffled slowly to rejoin their fellow inmates, an achingly slow gait due to a variety of broken bones. Some of the girls helped them walk, despite their manly protests.

We came back to the locked door, with a sense of trepidation. I knew we had to complete the search, but the smell of rot seemed to come from this area. I picked the lock in no time and threw the door wide open, trying to avert any attack. A swarm of flies were disturbed from the floor and I had to shoo them away to even see what I was dealing with.

I wish I hadn't. Bodies littered the dirt floor. All these men were worked so hard until their bodies gave out. The ones who had been dumped in the street or in the main compound were nothing compared to the sheer volume of death that lay before me. Several of the girls vomited, while I gagged as my stomach was already empty and throat raw. After ascertaining that there was no one alive in the room, I quietly closed the door. I had done all I could, but there were still so many dead. *Because of me.*

We quietly rejoined the rest of the men and took them to the temple. Those involved in the initial battle were starting to come to, no trace of the siren magick within their eyes. I sent fishnets out to collect Stevie and Damien; sure it was now safe for them to enter without being entranced. It was over.

Epilogue

In the aftermath of all that had happened, we found 102 men alive. Thirteen didn't make it through healthcare after their ordeal, succumbing to the wounds. There were 25 dead men found, and a few that were missing were never found. We searched after families pointed out that their men had never returned with the others but had to ultimately determine that they had been dumped in areas either not found, or too remote. The bloody snake disappeared and was never seen again. Part of me wondered if it was a spirit or a hallucination, but some of the other women reassured me that it had been there.

The black-haired siren? Yeah, I personally handed her over to Stevie. Street law took over the judgement there. With over 40 men dead or missing, Bette Lang didn't stand a chance.

I took some extra time to look into what made this situation, aided by Liselle and Sadie, who had suddenly taken an interest in spending more time at The Fox Den. Thanks to the public records shown to us by my grumpy fae librarian, we realised that Bette Lang, Sara Sweet and Norah Hall had all worked in the warehouses at the time of the spill.

When they lost their jobs due to the warehouses shutting down, they took to squatting in the abandoned warehouses. The contamination psychosis kept compounding over and over, until their mental health progressed to the point that they believed they were goddesses, and began to exploit their natural siren abilities. From there they had built up their drug fuelled cult.

I had taken to absorbing this kind of information gleefully. Stevie was ecstatic when I gave him the added details about why this incident had happened. He actually asked me to take it to Damien, with an odd little smile on his face.

'Ok, I will see if he is at his rooms,' I responded dubiously as I stood up and collected my precious notebook.

'Naw, I know where he be at. Ye get ter this address 'ere.' He slid a grubby page from a notebook across the table to me.

I was confused, but shrugged and started walking to the address given, roughly equally between The Fox Den and the Bayton Central Night Markets. Now that my little investigation was over, I guessed that Stevie would need the room again. Luckily from my work while I was still living there, I had a neat little stash of money, and a few pills here and there.

Even when we were doing the clean-up after the case, I was working at the K-Hole, so I had gotten a neat lil bit of change. The showers were definitely something I would miss though. Many nights I had sat in the shower and cried over shooting Sara Sweet. The bruises and fatigue had faded, but I was willing to bet that the tears from that one shot would be with me for a long time. Her name would be with me until I died.

Finally, I got to the address just as it began to sprinkle with rain. It was an odd little office, and I wondered what on earth Damien could want with it. It had a quirky business nature, rather than his usual retro-but-make-it-modern style. This was more a kind of Bohemian art deco, with patterned tiles and brass everywhere.

As I walked up the door opened, and Luis beckoned me in awkwardly. I shook the little drops of rain from my hair and saw Damien and... Jojo?

What on earth was Stevie's top man doing here with Damien? I looked between them, utterly confused and a little worried.

'Eh Jessie. Ye finished lookin' after dem missin' men nows. All wrapped up, yeh?' Damien asked ominously, stepping closer. The street sense in me had my heart in my throat and fear drumming at my brain.

Had I said the wrong thing? Did I find out the wrong information? I hadn't said a word about the K-Hole sale or anything. My mind whirred with all the possibilities that could lead up to me being dead in a kitch little office. Perhaps I was considered a loose end between the two men.

'Ye hold out yer hand, yeh?' Damien growled the order. I looked at Jojo, who nodded with his usual stern face. Gulping down my fear, accepting my fate, I put out my hand and closed my eyes by reflex.

A musical chime preceded something cold in my hand. I cracked my eyes open. There was an odd bunch of keys. Keys seemed to be a weird thing to give a dead girl. Perhaps there was a message in that. Like they were the keys to the K-Hole and a lost deal or more expensive buying price. Gang leaders did weird shit at times.

'W-what is this for?' I asked, my voice made tiny from fear.

'Yer new office. Oh, and there be an apartment up dere.' Damien pointed at the ceiling. I wasn't sure I had heard him correctly.

'My office for what?'

'Well, if ye want ter continue yer investigatin', ye got an office an' home. Stevie and I done bought it 'tween us. Ye kin use it. But sometimes we need things investigatin' an' ye help us, yeh?'

His words were magickal. I looked from Damien, to Jojo, to Luis. My... office? An office and a home? I burst into tears, hurling myself at the men with arms wide. They spontaneously all freaked out, mutually uncomfortable with the cyclone of emotions coming at them. In the end I managed to throw myself on Damien, with one arm on Jojo.

'Can I bring Liselle and Sadie?' I was thinking that they would be perfect to help out. Liselle was a smart woman, and Sadie knew the streets well.

'Ye can bring whoever ye want. This be yer place now. There be a whole second room upstairs for anyone ye be wantin'. What ye gonna call yer investigatin' business?' he asked, clearly delighted at my joy.

'I think I know the perfect name. Dead Girl Detectives.' I grinned, struck by the moment. Confusion ran across Damien's face. The other two were perfectly blank.

'Ye sure that's what ye want?' he queried tactfully. I nodded frantically.

'Yeah, it's perfect,' I shouted, before bolting upstairs to look at my apartment.

If you enjoyed Jessie's story, she will be back! I have two other books planned for now! Please feel free to give reviews and the like and tag me @ysadora.writes on most platforms.

If you wish to join my street and hype team on Facebook, please email me at ysadora.writes@gmail.com for details.

Ysadora's Debut Novel-
Heaven for a Predator

Embrace vampire politics, blood feuds, and the hunted in Heaven for a Predator. Furii is a bounty hunter of the elite Hellstorm clan, tasked with hunting the poor starvation addled bastards known as autophages. Those who feed on themselves. They are mindless creatures, vicious and stronger than the average vampire. Then, one of her bounties introduces herself. Autophages don't talk. Yet the sheriff insists she must die. Can Furii kill a sentient being?

What will Furii do when her whole perception of the world is turned on its head? And why is the deadly Duchess Du Mort sending her e-mails?

Furii must fight her way across the wasteland to save a tribe from extinction and rescue a man in distress, while in the shadows lurk autophages and bandits alike who want her dead.

Ysadora's First Series-
The Bayton Agency

Newly graduated law enforcement Agent, Tessa Bale is a witch. Upon surviving her low-paying internship and a sleazy boss, she is handed the most gruesome magickal murder case that could be found.

Succeeding won't be easy, pitting Tessa against the most vicious creatures magick can create while traversing the slums of Bayton. To survive, she will be forced to make an alliance with a mysterious demon.

Everything about Lee is forbidden. He's an efficient killer, addictively alluring, and holds powerful magick. Yet, what terrifies Tessa most is not the blood connection they now share, but that she finds herself oddly drawn to him.

But with a serial murderer on the loose, literal zombies walking the streets, and a brutal gang ex-lover on the rampage, Tessa must use every trick in her arsenal if she hopes to see the dawn.

Lady Tessa Bale still bears the physical and emotional scars from her first case when a new case is thrust upon her, as bloody and vicious as the last.

With one of the most famous witches in the area now a bloody mess on the floor of her kitchen, carved up with an array of occult sigils, Tessa must move quickly to appease the public. When the second body appears, this time a non-magickal person, all Hel breaks loose. The people of Bayton are quick to ire, and the fires of ill will are stoked by the local tabloids.

Tessa must balance her gruesome investigation while hiding one of the biggest secrets of her life. A secret she would die for. Unfortunately, a massive obsidian horned demon with a brutal reputation is all too happy to make that come true.